JACK'S SECRET SUMMER

JACK RYDER

HODDER

HODDER CHILDREN'S BOOKS

First published in Great Britain in 2020 by Hodder and Stoughton

3 5 7 9 10 8 6 4

A CIP catalogue record for this book
is available from the British Library.

ISBN 978 1 44495 297 1

Printed and bound in Great Britain by Clays Ltd.

The paper and board used in this book are from
well-managed forests and other responsible sources.

Hodder Children's Books
An imprint of
Hachette Children's Group
Part of Hodder & Stoughton
Carmelite House
50 Victoria Embankment
London EC4Y 0DZ

An Hachette UK Company
www.hachette.co.uk

www.hachettechildrens.co.uk

To my mum

PROLOGUE

There is often a moment in a child's life when everything around them feels so marvellously wonderful and just absolutely … perfect.

If only there were an invention that could bottle up the memory of this moment. It could be kept on a shelf for years and years, like some exquisite perfume, and then one day be uncorked with a magnificent pop! You could simply wave the bottle beneath your nose and relive the moment all over again. Wouldn't that be splendid?

Now, I shouldn't really be telling you this … but such an invention does actually exist. In fact, it exists right here within the pages of this book. But like most of the wondrous treasures in this world, it has long been forgotten. Until now …

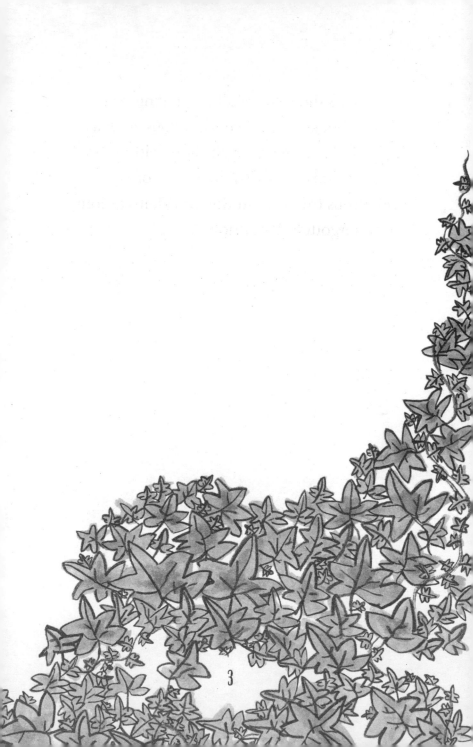

THE BOY ON THE HILL

It was the end of July and today was no ordinary day.

It was, in fact, a very special day indeed. A day that thousands of children all over the country had been dreaming about for many, many weeks and weeks. It was the last day of term and the summer holidays had finally arrived.

In a school in a small town at the bottom of a very big hill, a loud bell rang out. A moment later, hundreds of children came charging out through double doors, all screaming and laughing and hurling their bags up into the air. What a sight it was! With their arms stretched wide, every little girl and boy went soaring out of the school gates and into the open world, not once looking back.

However, there was one child among them who wasn't screaming or laughing or throwing his bag up into the air.

His name was Jack.

Jack lived at the top of the very big hill, and as he trudged his way up the slope towards his home it was clear he wasn't as excited about the summer holidays as the other children.

Up and up he climbed, dragging his feet as he went. The hill was so tall that whenever a heavy cloud floated by, all the little lanes would suddenly be blanketed in a magical fog and the houses would begin to disappear before your very eyes.

If you stood at the top of the hill and

looked down, you could see
far and wide over a beautiful
landscape of fields and forests. In
the distance, just under the horizon,
there was a lake and whenever the sun
hit it, the water would sparkle and shimmer
as if it were dancing. It was a magnificent
view from up there and the air was fresh
and clean.

But none of this cheered Jack as he
reached his home at the top of the hill.
And that was because Jack knew his
house would be empty.

Jack's mum wasn't around any more.
She had left when Jack was only three
years old. So Jack lived alone with his
dad, Mr Broom. But Mr Broom worked
hard, all day and most of the night, so Jack
didn't get to see much of him either.

Mr Broom worked at the Retirement
Home for Old Animals.

Exotic creatures were sent from all over the world to spend their final years at the animal home and it was Mr Broom's job to take care of them.

Mr Broom loved the animals, but it wasn't the animals that were the problem. The problem was Mr Broom's boss, Mr Nettles.

Mr Nettles was the grumpiest boss in the whole world. He detested his workers and made them stay late every night, the whole year round, and even on weekends.

Every morning, Mr Broom left the house at six o'clock on the dot and didn't arrive home again until long after dark. There were some nights when he didn't return home until after Jack's bedtime. On these occasions, Jack would make himself a jam sandwich for supper. After that, he would make another one for his father and leave

it on the table wrapped in
kitchen roll before going up to
bed.

Although Jack missed his father
very much, it wasn't all bad. He was
lucky in some ways, he told himself.

Being by himself at night meant that
Jack got to do things that other children
didn't. Such as turn the TV up really loud
or jump up and down on the bed. Jack
could stay up as late as he wanted, and
there was nobody there to tell him to
brush his teeth or go to bed.

But a lot of the time, Jack felt lonely,
and as he let himself into his house
on the last day of the summer term, he
couldn't help but wish there was someone
around to celebrate with.

The house was quiet as Jack turned the
key in the lock and let himself in. A sudden
sting of emptiness grabbed at his chest as

he kicked off his shoes. He left them by the front door and walked upstairs to his room.

He climbed on to his bed and lay there staring blankly up at the ceiling. The only sound was the faint ticking of the clock by Jack's bed.

He could feel himself longing for the simple pleasure of having another heartbeat in the house.

'Meowwww,' came a sound from the hallway.

'Ah, Ozzie,' said Jack, 'at least there's you, I suppose.'

Ozzie wasn't the best company, though. He was an old cat with long bushy white whiskers and most of his days were now spent sleeping under the radiator in the hall.

With a sigh, Jack turned over on to his side and stared at the wall next to his bed. It was covered with an enormous collage of postcards. There were hundreds of them, showing pictures of faraway places, sandy beaches, shining modern cities and colourful fields filled with beautiful flowers.

The postcards were from Jack's mum. Jack was too young to remember the day his mother had left. His father had told him she'd wanted to see the world. And so one day she'd packed her suitcase and flown off in a plane. Jack had never really known her, but he still missed her and always looked forward in a sad sort of way to a postcard landing on the doormat.

Just as the silence was beginning to close around him, Jack heard a thumping sound coming from the other side of the wall behind his head.

THUMP THUMP THUMP.

Jack sat bolt upright on his bed.

A loud voice from behind the wall

shouted, 'That's *disgusting*, Rocco. *Get out of my room!*'

This was followed by laughter and more thumping.

Even through the wall the shouts were deafening. Jack felt a little thrill of excitement. He slipped off his bed, pulled his window open and looked out.

That same moment, the window to his right was thrown open, and a scruffy head appeared, shortly followed by a body, which clambered out through the window and sat itself down on the window ledge. Its owner was a grubby little thing. His spindly legs were covered in crusts of dry mud and blades of grass were sticking out of his ears. His face was crinkled up in a frown, and he was wafting his hand in front of his nose, as if something in his room had gone off.

Jack was about to go back inside – he didn't want to look as if he was spying on him – when the boy looked over in his direction and grinned.

'All right?' he said, swinging his legs over the ledge.

'Hello,' said Jack a little shyly. Jack had met Bruno and his little brother Rocco a couple of times before, but never for very long. They had only moved in recently, and they always seemed to be wrapped up in some private game. Jack felt a bit awkward whenever he saw them, unsure if he should say hello or just leave them to it.

'Mum's gone to get us a takeaway!' said Bruno excitedly.

The thought of food hadn't crossed Jack's mind since he had arrived home from school, but now his stomach rumbled hungrily.

'And guess what else!' said Bruno, beckoning to Jack to come closer. 'I've got even *better* news …'

He was rubbing his hands together and grinning with the look of someone who had just come up with an evil plan.

Jack pushed his window open as wide as it would go and carefully swung out first one leg then another so he was sitting on his window ledge too.

But before Bruno got a chance to say more, another head appeared in the window next to Bruno's.

'Hello,' said Rocco, looking over at Jack with a grin. Rocco had messy hair and sticky-out ears and was wearing nothing but a baseball cap and a pair of bright red underpants.

'I said, *get out of my room, Rocco*!' Bruno ordered. 'Or I'll tell Mum you ate all her special chocolates!'

'I did not!' Rocco shouted.

'Then what's all that over your face?'

Rocco's eyes crossed as they tried to peer down at the smudges of melted chocolate smeared all over his chin. He grinned sheepishly.

'You are such a thief!' shouted Bruno. '*And* you nicked my favourite bed covers!'

Rocco frowned in confusion. 'What covers?'

'My space covers! They were my favourite! They glow in the dark and everything. Where have you hidden them?'

'I didn't steal your stupid space covers!' Rocco shouted. 'I don't even like space!'

'*Everyone* likes space.'

'Well, I don't!' said Rocco stubbornly.

Jack couldn't help smiling. He wasn't used to these sorts of sibling squabbles, having never had a brother or a sister himself. But he didn't mind it. In fact, he thought it looked like fun, having someone to bicker with.

He decided, however, that this might be a good moment to change the subject, before things got more heated.

'Um, what were you going to say before?' Jack asked Bruno.

'When?' said Bruno.

'Some good news, you said …'

'Oh yeah!' Bruno replied cheerily. 'Get this – Mum and Dad are going away! Something about their soppy wedding anniversary. They'll be gone for three whole days! Do you know what that means?'

Bruno and Rocco looked at each other and mischievous smiles spread across their faces.

'No parents means … no rules!' said Rocco, and Jack burst out laughing as Rocco started tap dancing madly across the bedroom floor.

'We're gonna have some fun tomorrow, Jacky-boy!' said Bruno, jumping down to join his brother in his silly dance. 'Come over, if you like?'

Jack's heart swelled with joy at the invitation. Before he could reply, a loud voice shouted up from below. 'What are you two doing up there? Your food's getting cold!'

'*Takeaway!*' screamed the brothers.

'See you tomorrow, Jack!' shouted Bruno

over his shoulder as he and Rocco went tearing out of the room and down the stairs for dinner.

And Jack was alone again. But this time he felt a little less lonely. He swung his legs contentedly and looked out at the view. From up here he could see all the way across his and next-door's back gardens, to the alley behind, and the old empty house that his granddad used to live in. And beyond that to the left, he could see right down the hill to the town below, the lights all twinkling on as the sun began to set.

Jack smiled to himself as he thought again of Bruno's words … *We're gonna have some fun tomorrow, Jacky-boy!*

Perhaps the summer holidays weren't going to be so bad after all …

19

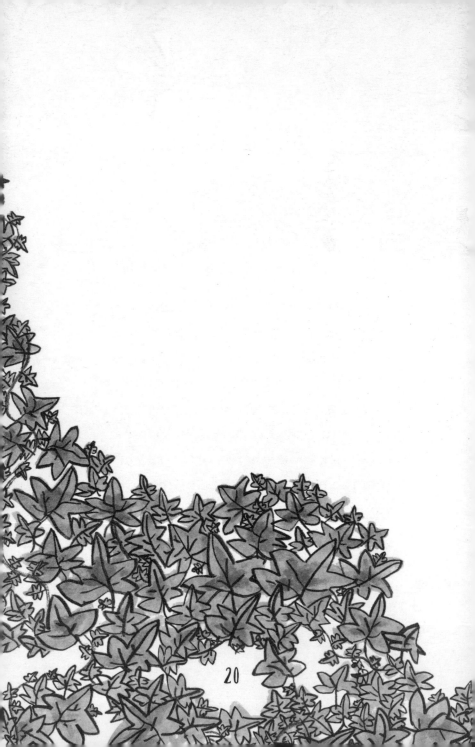

20

BEAN JUICE

It was around nine o'clock in the morning when Jack rolled over and peered at his bedside clock.

Muffled cries from next door had been rumbling through the wall for over an hour now, drifting in and out of Jack's dreams. Then Jack remembered Bruno's invitation from the night before, and he threw the covers off and leapt excitedly out of bed.

A loud banging that sounded to Jack like a heavy suitcase being thrown downstairs could only mean one thing – Bruno and Rocco's parents were already leaving!

Jack got dressed in a hurry and tore down the stairs. What fantastic and dangerous plans the brothers had come up with, Jack could only imagine. Their playing always looked wild to Jack, even when their parents *were* there. The sheer thought of the fun ahead made his tummy do somersaults.

Jack came bursting out of his house and hopped over the low wall into next-door's front garden. The air was warm and the sun was shining brightly over the hill as Jack knocked on the door.

When the front door finally opened, a dog came bounding straight at Jack, tail wagging furiously.

She was a white spaniel, with long flappy ears and furry brown patches all over. She curled her wriggling back excitedly into Jack's shins as her tail went thumping against the ground like a beating drumstick.

Jack smiled and gave her a good old scratch behind the ear.

Behind the dog was Bruno and Rocco's mum, Mrs Buckley.

She was already wearing her gigantic sunglasses and was fiddling around for something in her handbag.

Mrs Buckley was a tiny woman with wild blonde hair and huge hooped earrings that were almost as big as her head.

'Hello, love,' said Mrs Buckley. 'Jack, isn't it? I see you've met Dottie. Boys, your friend's here!' she called out over her shoulder. 'We're off now!'

She smiled at Jack before suddenly screaming out, 'Are you boys listening to me?'

Mr Buckley collected the suitcase from the bottom of the stairs and started hauling it out to the car, giving Jack a firm nod on his way past.

'Now don't forget,' Mrs Buckley shouted, 'your Aunt Nora will be here soon!'

A loud groan came from the doorway where Bruno and Rocco had appeared.

'You never told us that stupid Aunt Nora was looking after us,' Bruno grumbled.

'We can take care of ourselves, you know!' said Rocco.

'We'll have less of that chat, thank you very much,' Mrs Buckley replied hotly. 'And I don't want any funny business while your dad and I are away. Understood?'

Bruno and Rocco mumbled under their breath in reply.

Mrs Buckley smiled and pointed a finger at each cheek. 'Now, give your mum a kiss.'

The brothers begrudgingly came forward and each pecked at a cheek.

'Good boys,' she said. Then with a wave and a smile, Mrs Buckley jumped in the car

24

next to her husband and a second later they were tearing off down the lane.

'Right,' Bruno said, rubbing his hands together gleefully. 'Follow me.'

Jack followed the brothers through the kitchen and out into the back garden. Dottie leapt out after them on to the patio and started sniffing at the grass busily.

'Let the battles commence!' cried Rocco.

He motioned proudly to the wall where a large glass bowl, a wooden spoon and eight cans of kidney beans were sitting, all lined up neatly in a row. Jack noticed Rocco had tied a red bandana around his head. He looked as though he was going to war.

'Are you ready?' Rocco said to his brother.

'What's happening?' asked Jack excitedly.

'I've bet Bruno that he can't eat all these kidney beans in under five minutes!'

'The whole eight cans?' said Jack, shocked.

'Yep,' Rocco said, grinning. 'And if he loses, he has to give me all his pocket money for the rest of the year! I'm saving up for a new BMX!'

Jack could see a sense of glory glistening in Rocco's eyes, as if he had already won the bet.

'And what if Bruno wins?' Jack asked, though he thought that was very unlikely.

'Then Rocco has to eat anything *I* tell him to,' Bruno said.

'As long as it's edible!' Rocco snapped. 'And nothing out of date …' he added as he began pouring the tins of purply coloured kidney beans into the glass bowl.

Bruno nodded, though Jack noticed he looked a little uneasy.

'What's all that wet stuff?' asked Bruno, frowning.

26

'It's bean juice!' Rocco chuckled. 'Having second thoughts, are we? Don't think you can take it?'

Bruno just ignored him and started bouncing up and down on his toes, throwing punches into the air like a boxer.

When the final can was empty, Rocco rubbed his hands together and Bruno took in a long deep breath.

It was time to begin.

The large glass bowl was now filled to the top with a mountain of wet, slippery kidney beans. Rocco unstrapped his watch and placed it on the wall.

Bruno leaned forward over the bowl, wooden spoon clenched in his fist. He suddenly looked a bit queasy.

'Are you sure this is a good idea?' asked Jack.

'Don't you worry, Jacky-boy!' said Bruno. 'Piece of cake!'

With narrowed eyes, Rocco focused carefully on the watch and raised his arm into the air.

There was a moment's deathly silence.

Then Rocco's arm came swooshing down as he roared, '*Go!*'

At the same moment, Bruno tossed the wooden spoon over his shoulder and instead plunged both his hands into the bowl of beans. He began shovelling huge handfuls of the stuff into his mouth, chomping away louder than a T. rex. He chomped and chewed and slurped while all the time crushing the beans inside his fists with a *SPLAT*! This turned half the beans he was devouring into a mushy paste which made it a lot easier to guzzle down.

Rocco's devilish grin slowly began to fall from his face as reality dawned on him – Bruno was already halfway through and they hadn't even reached the second minute!

Bruno munched away at an even more ferocious speed as he tried a new tactic and plunged his entire head into the bowl. He was stuffing his face like a pig in a trough. Then in a final triumphant move, Bruno picked up the bowl, tipped the rest of the contents into his mouth … and he was done.

Jack leapt into the air with a cheer. 'That was incredible!' he cried. 'I can't believe you did it! And with a whole minute left on the clock!'

Bruno looked up at Rocco and proudly licked his lips. His whole face was smeared with bean juice. It was all in his hair and smudged into his forehead. He looked like he had just been scribbled on by a baby with a purple crayon. Then he smiled at his brother, with purple teeth, and rubbed his belly.

'So I guess that means you have to eat whatever I tell you to?' said Bruno as he wiped the oily bean juice from his chin and strolled off down the garden, adding, 'Come with me.'

Rocco kicked the ground furiously, then followed Bruno across the grass. Bruno stopped next to a small pond. He stood on the edge of it with his fists punched against his hips like he was Superman. For a moment it looked as though he was about to dive in but then he pointed into the water.

'One of those,' he said.

Rocco and Jack peered into the pond. As far as Jack could see, it was completely empty.

'One of what?' Rocco asked.

'One of *those*!' said Bruno in a much firmer tone, his purple-stained finger still pointing at the pond. The boys crouched down to get a closer look.

Through the murky water they could see a swarm of freshwater worms all wriggling and squiggling about beneath the surface.

'Worms?' Jack said, horrified.

'Yes,' said Bruno. 'That is what Rocco's going to eat.'

Rocco leapt back in fright. 'Worms!?' he shrieked, his face turning white.

'Yep!' said Bruno.

'I'm not eating a worm! They're disgusting and slimy!'

Bruno dunked his hand into the pond and sifted it round and round like a net through the water.

'Yes, you are. You are going to eat a worm,' he said firmly. 'They're not out of date, they're completely edible and that was the bet.'

'Worms don't *have* a date, though,'

protested Rocco as he marched away from the pond in an explosive huff. He was pacing up and down the garden, shaking his head from side to side.

'Exactly!' said Bruno. 'So they can't be *out* of date!' Then with a loud 'Gotcha!' Bruno turned to Rocco, holding a fresh slippery worm between his fingers.

'I'm not doing it!' Rocco barked.

Bruno shook the silky water from his hand and calmly walked up to Rocco. 'Well, then *you* have to give *me* all your pocket money for the rest of the year! And also – I'm the winner, and you're the *loser*.'

They were face to face now.

'You're not a *loser*, are you, Rocco?' Bruno said quietly.

Rocco didn't move as he eyeballed his older brother.

Jack was staring at them both with wide eyes, wondering what on earth was going to happen. It didn't seem too far a stretch to imagine that Rocco would do it, Jack thought to himself. Jack had looked down from his bedroom window not long ago to see Rocco pick a crinkly old bogey out of his nose and gobble it up as if it were a fresh strawberry.

The brothers were staring hard at each other now. Jack watched them closely. The tension in the air could be popped with a pin.

Rocco said nothing for a moment longer and then the doomed look in his eyes started to change. A new confidence was rising inside him, Jack could tell. Jack could see that there was no way in hell Rocco was going to let his older brother win. Bruno seemed to notice the look too and a flicker of doubt flashed across his face. Was this some kind of bluff?

But no. With narrowing eyes,

Rocco nodded at his brother. Challenge accepted.

Bruno held his fist out under Rocco's nose and slowly opened his hand.

Inside it lay a long, slimy worm. It was wriggling away, and Jack had to gulp down a wave of nausea just looking at it.

'If you just swallow it whole, it might be OK,' Jack said feebly, trying to lend some moral support.

Rocco was staring at the worm as if hypnotised by a spell.

'It's now or never,' Bruno said calmly.

Then in a flash Rocco pinched the fleshy worm out of his brother's hand, tilted his head back and dropped it into his mouth like a strand of spaghetti.

A twinkle of light sparkled off the worm's silky tail as it fell through the air, and the only sound that followed was an enormous gulp.

Jack was half expecting Rocco to drop dead on the spot from worm poisoning, but this didn't happen. Instead it was Bruno who dropped to the ground. He fell to his knees and started pounding the grass with his fists.

Suddenly, from nowhere, there came a screeching voice.

'Ah, there you are, my little cherubs!'

The boys all looked up. There on the patio was the strangest-looking woman Jack had ever seen.

THE HULA HOOPING MANIAC!

The woman was as thin as a lamp post with huge bush-like hair and dressed from head to toe in neon Lycra. But it wasn't what she was wearing that was so strange. It was what she was carrying. Because along both arms, from shoulders to wrists, the woman was strung with hula hoops. She must have been carrying a hundred of them, all different sizes, and all brightly coloured neon like her outfit. She could barely stand straight from the weight of them.

She stood there beaming at the boys.

'Is that your aunt?' whispered Jack out

of the side of his mouth.

'Yeah, that's her,' Rocco muttered under his breath.

Aunt Nora came down the steps towards them, dragging her hula hoops with her. When she reached the bottom, she dropped them all on the grass, kicked off her neon pink trainers and began twirling around the garden like she was dancing at a grand ball.

'Oh, how I love the fresh air!' she sang. 'There is so much more space out here. It is the perfect place for me to continue my training. I need to be at the very peak of my athletic abilities at the moment. I'm sure your mother's told you about my record-breaking talent?'

The boys all stared at her in stunned silence, the only sound a quiet gurgle from Bruno's stomach.

Aunt Nora stared at them expectantly until Jack couldn't bear it any more. 'Is it …

hula hooping?' he asked.

'It is, yes, it is! Oh, it's really quite something,' she whispered excitedly. 'This is sure to be an enlightening time for us all. Let me show you.'

Bruno's stomach rumbled again. It was louder this time, like the rumbling of distant thunder.

They all watched slack-jawed as Aunt Nora grabbed the pile of hula hoops from the ground, threw them over her head and limbs and began gyrating like a deranged person. A surge of colourful rings whirled all around her. They were spinning around her waist. They were spinning around her arms. Three of them were spinning around her neck!

'I've been practising for months!' she cried out through gritted teeth. 'It really is quite invigorating!'

Jack couldn't tell whether she was

enjoying the experience or finding the whole thing rather painful. It looked as if she was being tortured.

All at the same time, her body was jerking back and forth while her hips were wiggling from side to side. She was putting a great amount of concentration into it and it was clear that she was taking the world of hula hooping very seriously.

She came spinning towards them, crying out, 'I'm attempting the world record, my dears! Another thirty hoops and I'll be a world-record breaker!'

She was shaking uncontrollably now and that was when Jack noticed Bruno. He was clutching at his stomach, with a pained look on his face. His legs were writhing and twisting together, as if they were trying to keep something in.

From the depths of Bruno's body came another deep rumble, like a gurgling volcano. And then it erupted.

PARRRRRRRP!

There was nothing to stop it. It was without doubt the almightiest fart Jack had ever heard in his life. It was so loud that all the little birds suddenly flew out of the trees as if a foghorn had gone off.

Aunt Nora stopped spinning. Her hoops fell to the floor and then she slowly lifted her nostrils into the air.

'Urgggh!' She quivered as her nose twitched in revulsion. 'Smells like an animal died. You DISGUSTING boy!'

Bruno burst out laughing and Jack was trying as hard as he could not to do the same when he caught sight of Rocco.

Rocco had been standing right next to his brother at the time of the eruption, and Jack could now see this had taken its toll. Rocco had in fact turned completely green, and was desperately trying to waft the evil stench away from his face.

'Are you OK?' Jack whispered to him.

'I'm fine,' Rocco mumbled, and for a moment he seemed to get control. Then he lurched forward, clutching his tummy, and threw up. All over Aunt Nora's bare feet.

For a moment, the garden was completely silent.

Then Aunt Nora's eyes began to twitch as she stared in horror at … a worm. It was writhing and curling itself between her now sticky toes.

She grasped her throat with a shaking hand and it looked almost as if she was strangling herself. The boys started backing away, sensing something was about to happen, but it was too late. All of a sudden Aunt Nora leapt into the air, kicking the worm from her feet as though a bomb had exploded beneath her … and she began to scream.

'You DISGUSTING LITTLE MONSTERS!' she howled in a fit of horror. 'You filthy BEASTS! Get out of my sight! Go and play where I can't see you! And take that HORRIBLE dog with you!'

The boys grabbed Dottie, who was helpfully trying to lick Aunt Nora's toes clean, and ran off to the bottom of the garden and out of the gate, shouting, 'Sorry!' over their shoulders.

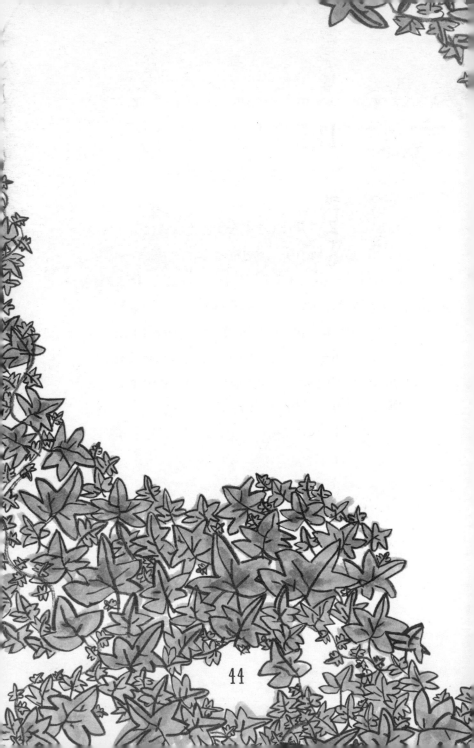

THE OLD EMPTY HOUSE

'Don't know what all the fuss is about,' said Rocco, smirking, as the boys made it to the safety of the little alley behind the gardens. 'At least she didn't have to eat it like I did!'

The day was getting hotter and Jack wiped the sweat from the back of his neck as he tried to shake the image of the soggy worm wrapped around Aunt Nora's toes from his mind. As the boys trundled down the alley, wispy clouds drifted by blanketing them with some welcome shade.

'Are you feeling better now?' asked Jack,

45

unsure which of the brothers he was asking.

Bruno rubbed his stomach and grinned. 'Much better, thanks.'

'What are we going to do now?' said Rocco.

'Can't believe we've been banned from our own garden,' grumbled Bruno.

Rocco stopped next to a ladder that was leaning against the tall wall on the other side of the alley. Behind the wall was an old abandoned house, the one that Jack's granddad used to live in, which he could see from his bedroom window. The house had stood empty for a while now. It was completely run-down and overgrown with ivy.

A slow smile spread across Rocco's face. 'Dare you to climb over!' he said to Bruno.

'No way,' said Bruno. 'I heard ghosts live in there!'

'Or maybe thieves!' said Rocco. 'Hiding

out till they do their next job!'

Jack didn't feel scared of the old house. To him it just looked sad and empty. A feeling of bravery grew inside him. He knew this was a chance to impress the brothers.

'I'll do it!' he said.

The brothers turned to him with looks of admiration on their faces. Jack had never been looked at that way before, and it made him feel braver.

'Go on, Jacky-boy!' said Bruno, giving him a bump on the shoulder. 'Didn't know you had it in you!'

Jack looked up at the old house and took a deep breath. There was no going back now. Before he could think better of it, he darted up the ladder.

What he saw when he got to the top almost took his breath away. Stretching out beneath him was a wild jungle – a garden so vast and overgrown it seemed endless.

Beyond it was the strange house itself. It didn't look like any of the other houses on the hill. You could barely see any bricks, or any windows, there was no front door in sight, no chimney with an aerial sticking out of the top. All these things were completely hidden from view and buried under what was now a mountain of tangled vines and thousands upon thousands of shiny green ivy leaves all wrapped around each other a million times.

Jack felt a little sad staring at the house, all empty and abandoned. He waited there at the top of the ladder, listening for some kind of sound, but nothing came.

'Go on then, climb over!' said Bruno gleefully.

'I don't know if he should …' said Rocco, a slight waver to his voice.

'Are you *scared*?' said Bruno, poking his brother.

'N-no,' said Rocco, but Jack had to admit there was a spooky feeling in the air surrounding the house.

'I wonder why no one's ever bought it?' said Rocco.

'Well, would *you* want to live there?' said Bruno.

Rocco kept silent for a few seconds then cried out, 'Maybe whoever lived there died and there's a body inside!'

'A body?' Bruno scoffed.

'A *dead* body,' Rocco said darkly. 'Probably be a rotten skeleton by now.'

'No one's lived there since my

granddad,' Jack said. 'So no dead bodies. I guess it just went wild and then no one wanted to buy it.'

The brothers were silenced by this piece of information.

'What can you see, anyway?' asked Rocco.

'It's … it's amazing,' said Jack. 'It's like a jungle.'

Bruno and Rocco looked at each other, then suddenly they both scrambled up the ladder behind Jack. They peered over the top of the wall and gasped.

'Whoa!' said Rocco.

'I wish our garden was all wild like that!' said Bruno.

'I don't know,' said Rocco. 'It looks creepy.'

'So are you going over then?' said Bruno, slapping Jack on the back.

But before Jack could reply, a high-pitched scream and several loud barks came ringing out from the Buckleys' back garden. The boys all looked at each other.

'Where's Dottie?' said Rocco.

'GET THIS ANIMAL OFF ME!' came the shrill cries of Aunt Nora.

'I guess that's your answer,' said Bruno. The boys scrambled back down the ladder, falling the last few steps and landing on top of each other with a thud.

They quickly picked themselves up and ran towards the house to find out what all the fuss was about.

As they burst back through the garden gate, they came to a shuddering halt. Aunt Nora was wrestling with Dottie on the patio. Dottie's hind legs were swinging through the air, her teeth clamped down on one of Aunt Nora's spinning hula hoops which the crazed aunt was desperately trying to wrestle back from her.

She began slapping at Dottie to try to shoo her away but Dottie's jaw was locked down so tightly, even a crowbar would have had trouble prising it open.

'Get off! Get OFF!' Aunt Nora was yelling. 'You're going to break my hoop! Boys! Get this foul beast away from me!'

Jack walked towards the shrieking woman, wondering if he could encourage Dottie away somehow, but there was no

way she was going to let go of her new
toy. Jack looked over to the Buckleys
for help, but they were shrieking with
laughter and clearly had no intention
of helping their aunt, who was now
being dragged across the lawn on her
backside. Jack leapt out of the way as
she came sliding past him with her
arms waving about in the air.

'HELP ME!' Aunt Nora screamed.

Then, suddenly, the hula hoop in
Dottie's jaw snapped apart and both aunt
and dog went flying backwards away from
each other.

Everything came to a grinding stop as
Aunt Nora hit the grass with an almighty
bump. The garden fell eerily silent. Aunt
Nora didn't move. She just stayed there,
very still, her whole body lying flat out on
the lawn.

'How are you doing there, Aunt Nora?'

asked Rocco as he crept closer and stood over her. Jack could see how hard he was trying to contain his laughter. It looked as if it almost hurt.

Aunt Nora sat up and eyeballed first Rocco, then Bruno, then Jack. Her face had all swelled up like an angry blowfish, her hair now wilder than ever.

'This dog …' she uttered in a dangerously low voice as she pointed a shaking finger at Dottie, 'is *banned* from the house! How dare it destroy my favourite, prize-winning hula hoop! I will not let this disgusting mutt ruin my chances of breaking a world record!'

The boys were watching her open-mouthed as she gathered up her hula hoops, which were now splayed out all over the garden as if they had come raining down from the sky.

Then she stumbled breathlessly towards

the house, hula hoops hanging off her arms, and shouted back, 'That dog's staying out here! I won't have it in the house!'

'You can't do that!' Rocco cried.

'I can do whatever I like!' she said with narrowing eyes. 'And you boys go to your room. NOW!'

The brothers looked at each other dumbstruck. Then they went over to Dottie, who was happily chewing on her new hula hoop toy, and gave her a pat on the head. 'There's a good dog,' said Bruno under his breath. 'We won't let you stay out here for long, I promise.'

And with a shrug at Jack, the brothers shuffled off reluctantly towards the house.

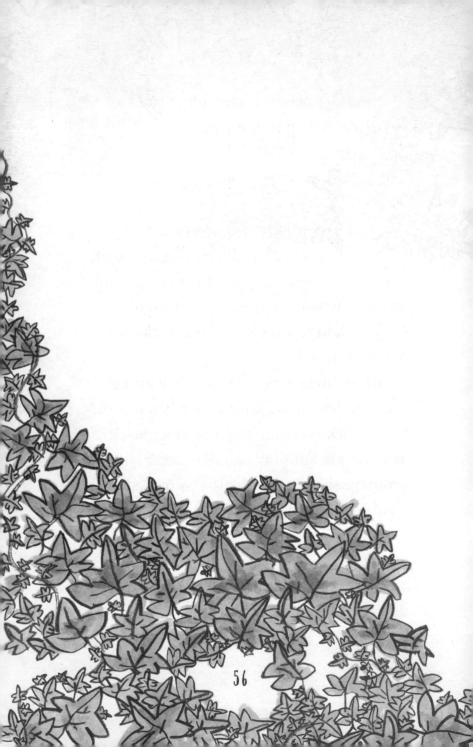

BEDTIME

It was late when the howling started.

Jack had just flicked off his socks and jumped into bed.

Ozzie the cat was snoring like an old man under the radiator in the hall as usual.

As Jack lay there in the warm glow of his bedside lamp, the terrible noise rose up from outside. It was the sound of an animal in great distress, and Jack couldn't bear to hear it.

He jumped up from his bed and looked through the window down into the Buckleys' garden.

Through the darkness he could just
make out Dottie. She was tied to a tree
at the far end of the garden, and was
lying slumped on the ground. Jack felt
enormously sorry for the poor creature
being out there all alone. He wished he
could bring her home with him, but Ozzie
would never stand for it.

'We'll save you, Dottie, don't worry,' Jack
whispered through the window. He didn't
know how yet, but he would figure out a
way.

Jack was so focused on poor Dottie
that he didn't hear the footsteps on the
stairs and he jumped as the bedroom door
suddenly swung open. He turned to see a
long black figure standing in the doorway. It
was Jack's father, Mr Broom.

'Oh, I do love a jam sandwich,' his
dad said through a smile and a mouthful
of crumbs.

'Hi, Dad,' said Jack, his face breaking into a smile too.

'I thought you'd be asleep,' Mr Broom said, stepping into the room in his heavy boots. 'I came to check you were all right. I was being as quiet as I could.'

Mr Broom finished the last mouthful of his sandwich and came to join Jack at the window. 'What's that terrible noise?' he asked as Dottie started howling again.

'Bruno and Rocco's aunt has come to stay,' he explained, 'and she doesn't seem to like dogs much.'

'Oh dear,' chuckled Mr Broom. 'Poor thing.'

One of the things Jack loved most about his father was his laugh. Even after the longest and hardest of days, his father would almost always share a smile and a joke with Jack at the end of it. And even if he couldn't form a smile with his mouth, he would always smile at him softly with his eyes.

'That sandwich was great, thanks very much,' said Mr Broom. 'I haven't eaten all day.' As Jack got back into bed, his dad dragged over a small wooden chair and sat beside him.

'Not even lunch?' Jack asked.

'You know what grumpy Nettles is like,' said his dad with a thin smile. 'Still, I work for him and he pays me so I get on with it and do as I'm told. Never let a grudge stop you from doing good work, Jack.'

Jack nodded to his father. He always listened attentively when his dad gave him advice.

'So, it's your first day of the holidays,' Mr Broom said, then leaning in closer, he added, 'What mischief have you been getting up to, then?'

'You'll never guess what happened today,' Jack said with a playful grin. And he told him about the Buckleys' crazy bets and Rocco swallowing a worm and then throwing up all over Aunt Nora's feet.

Mr Broom leaned all the way back in his chair, laughing his head off. He eventually came forward again, slapping his hands down on his knees. 'Sounds like a good day then, son,' he said, wiping the tears from his eyes. 'I'm sorry I wasn't there to see it.'

There was a short silence as Jack thought about the old abandoned house.

'Right,' Mr Broom said, stretching his arms out as far as he could. 'I think it's time for us to get some sleep.'

He kissed Jack goodnight and as he walked to the door, Jack said, 'What happened to Granddad's old house?'

Mr Broom stopped and turned.

'I mean, how come no one's ever bought it?' Jack added.

'I don't know, Jack,' Mr Broom said quietly. 'It's not really fit for living in now, I guess.'

'But why did no one else live there after Granddad?'

There was another pause. 'Well, it was a strange old house and your granddad was a strange old man.'

'Strange in what way?' Jack asked him.

'Oh, I don't know, Jack. Just strange,' said his dad with a sigh. 'Come on now, it's late. Time to sleep.'

Jack wanted to know more but he knew his dad worked hard and must be tired. He decided not to press him any more for tonight.

'Good night, Jack,' said Mr Broom. 'Oh, did you see the new postcard? I put it on your stool,' he added, before closing the door softly.

Jack reached over and held his mother's postcard under the light of his lamp.

On the front of the card was a picture of the Eiffel Tower in Paris. Jack turned the card over and inspected the writing on the other side. It was addressed to him and it said:

Dear Jack,

Thinking of you every day. I hope the sun in England is warm and bright.

Mum x x x

Jack kissed the back of the card, returned it to the stool and switched off the light.

He lay there a while, thinking about the

old empty house and listening to the sound
of Dottie's howls in the distance, before
eventually falling asleep.

MIDNIGHT PLAN

When Jack came downstairs the next morning and turned on the radio in the kitchen, the news was all abuzz with talk of a big storm. It was soon to be coming in from somewhere over the North Atlantic and would bring with it a month's worth of rain in one day.

Poor Dottie, Jack thought as he went back up to his room to get dressed. He decided to pop round to see how Bruno and Rocco were getting on with Aunt Nora.

The howling had stopped now, and so had the rain, but if a big storm was coming, they couldn't just leave Dottie outside to fend for herself. He knew how scared animals could be by thunder and lightning, and this storm sounded like it would bring plenty of that.

As he came out of his front door and hopped over the little wall that separated his and the Buckleys' front gardens, he was met by a very strange sight.

There was a huge pile of furniture stacked up in the front garden. Chairs and tables were all piled on top of each other, and even the sofa was out there.

Perhaps Bruno and Rocco are building a camp? he thought. Had they decided to get away from their aunt by living outside instead?

He stepped over a floor lamp that was lying on its side and banged on the front door.

It was a few minutes before the door swung open and a hand reached out, yanking him inside.

Bruno swiftly marched Jack up the stairs and shoved him through a door into his bedroom. Rocco was in there too, looking forlorn on the bed.

'What's going on?' said Jack.

'Shhhh!' Bruno hissed, pressing his finger hard against his lips.

Bruno pushed Jack out of the way and walked over to a large chest of drawers. Dragging it across the carpet, he wedged it firmly against the door, then turned back to Jack and whispered, 'We need to do something!'

'What's happened?' asked Jack. 'Why's all the furniture outside?'

'She's crazy!' said Bruno, pacing around the room. 'She's only put all our furniture outside to make room for her stupid hula hoop training! She's taken over the whole house!'

'*And* she won't let Dottie back in,' grumbled Rocco.

Jack was speechless. 'But … can't you do anything? Call your parents or something?'

'Oh yeah,' Bruno said, glaring at Jack. 'Great idea. Then we'd get in trouble with them too for making Aunt Nora angry in the first place. No, we're going to have to deal with this ourselves.' He cracked his knuckles, and carried on pacing restlessly round the room.

'The mad bat even put the TV out there!' said Rocco grumpily.

'You can both watch TV at mine if you want?' Jack said rather feebly.

'Forget about the TV!' said Bruno. 'First thing we need to do is find a safe place for Dottie.'

'Is she still tied up out there?' Jack asked. He went over to the window and, sure enough, there was poor Dottie, tied to a tree, looking very lonely and forlorn.

'She's OK for now,' Bruno said, keeping his voice down. 'I sneaked out first thing this morning and gave her some food. But we need to find her somewhere to stay before that storm arrives.'

'What shall we do?'

There was silence while the three boys considered their options.

'Can you take her to yours?' asked Rocco hopefully.

'I'm sorry,' Jack said sadly. 'My cat would scratch Dottie's eyes out if she came into the house.'

The boys slumped into silence again. Jack could see the desperation in the brothers' eyes as they racked their brains as to what to do. He hated seeing his friends like this.

Jack looked out of the window again. Thick grey clouds were forming in the sky.

They were so low you could almost touch them and all the tops of the houses were beginning to disappear. In the distance, beyond the Buckleys' garden wall, Jack could just see the top of the old empty house, clouds curling round the ivy.

Suddenly he had a fantastic and marvellous idea. It was also a crazy one.

'Um, I know what we could do,' Jack said, unsure whether he should say the words or not. 'We could keep her in the old empty house.'

There was a moment's silence while they all considered this possibility.

'Yes, Jacky-boy!' Bruno said, a smile spreading across his face. 'We'll just sneak her in. It's perfect! We won't have to stay there long. Then at least she'll have shelter from the rain.'

There was definitely something scary about the old empty house – even the

thought of stepping inside
it made all the little hairs on
Jack's arms stand on end. But
Jack had to admit the plan was a
little bit exciting too. And anyway, they
couldn't just stand by and watch poor
Dottie spend another cold night locked
outside.

'Now,' Bruno said as he scratched his
head thoughtfully, making his hair go all
scruffy. 'How do we get inside? Do we just
go over the ladder?'

Jack thought about this. Though
the house was empty, it wasn't theirs
to break into, and he didn't want to
get spotted going in there by a nosy
neighbour, or worse – Aunt Nora.

Jack took a long deep breath and said,
'We'll have to go at night, so no one sees
us.'

Rocco looked a bit unsure, but Bruno

nodded. 'We'll do it tonight, when Aunt Nora's gone to sleep.'

'I can sneak out when Dad's gone to bed too,' said Jack.

'OK, what time shall we meet?'

Jack thought for a second and then with a shrug said, 'Midnight?'

'Perfect!' said Bruno, punching the air. 'Midnight it is!'

SNEAKING OUT

Human beings can do the strangest of things, and every once in a while a person who is normally quite timid or shy can be remarkably brave.

But at just before midnight, Jack wasn't feeling as bold as he had been that morning. In fact, if you were to ask him why exactly he'd chosen to enter a dark and empty house in the middle of the night, he probably wouldn't have been able to tell you. But there are moments in all our lives when one must be fearless and walk daringly into the unknown, and tonight was such a moment.

With a fluttering in his stomach, Jack slid out of bed and tiptoed down the stairs. He pulled his coat on over his pyjamas and carefully slipped his bare feet into some shoes, then stood listening for ten seconds or so. Had he woken his father? But the house was completely silent. Jack quietly crept out of the back door.

The night air was cool and not a sound could be heard.

The moon was beaming brightly like a gigantic torch in the night sky. It made everything under it look silvery and pale. Not a single car went by on the lane and not a footstep could be heard on the hill.

Jack scurried down to the bottom of the garden as quickly as he could. When he got to the gate that led into the alley behind, he turned and looked back at the house.

No light came on. He had done it. He

had sneaked out at night without waking his father.

Jack had never been out alone at such a late hour before and a nervous feeling started bouncing about like a pinball inside his stomach. But mixed in with that feeling was an undeniable thrill of excitement as he pushed open the gate, squeezed through the gap and stepped into the alley.

There were no street lamps along this quiet back alley, and all the windows of the houses whose gardens backed on to the alley were black. Everyone on the hill was asleep and Jack felt like the only boy in the world.

He looked around in the darkness but could see no sign of Bruno and Rocco yet. Jack suddenly had a terrible image of Aunt Nora locking the brothers in the house and hiding the key.

Then came a sound.

It was a tiny tinkling sound.

Jack knew instantly what it was.

It was the bell on Dottie's collar.

A moment later, barely visible among the long black shadows, Jack could just make out Dottie pushing her way through the Buckleys' gate. Even in the dark Jack could tell Dottie was wagging her tail. She bounded towards him and curled around his legs. Jack smiled and knelt down beside her as she leapt up at him and began flicking at his chin with her tongue. He patted her fur gently, trying to soften her excited cries, but she was too overcome with emotion.

'Shhh, Dottie,' Jack whispered, 'you'll get us caught!'

A moment later he heard the faint sound of human voices and Bruno and Rocco came through the gate after Dottie. They

76

were nattering away and squabbling with each other in not very quiet whispers.

'Great!' Bruno whispered when he spotted Jack. 'You're here already!'

Jack nodded a hello and straightened, dusting the alley's dirt off his knees.

Dottie was now so excited she was jumping up at the three of them with her wet paws.

'Right,' Jack whispered. 'Are we doing this then?' He hoped his voice sounded braver than he felt.

The three boys turned as one to look over at the empty house. In the moonlight, the ivy that covered not only the house but also the back wall of the alley seemed almost alive, as if it were crawling over the wall towards them.

'Let's do it,' said Bruno with a determined look in his eye. Then after another moment he said, 'Er, where's the ladder?'

'Someone's taken it!' said Rocco, looking around. 'Oh well, we'd better go back to bed ...' He sounded not at all unhappy at the idea.

'There must be a gate somewhere,' said Jack.

It was quite simple in Jack's mind. If *he* had a back gate at the bottom of his garden, and the Buckleys had a back gate at the bottom of theirs, then the old empty house – whose garden backed on to the opposite side of the alley to theirs – must have one too.

'It's probably just hidden by the leaves,' said Jack. The boys began examining the wall, feeling for any sign of a gate.

'Bingo!' came the voice of Bruno from up ahead, and Jack and Rocco rushed over. Sure enough, beneath the ivy was something hard and cold.

'Metal!' said Jack, and the boys all began pulling at the ivy, ripping great vines of it away from the metal below. Dottie was there too, sniffing and scratching at the ground, as if desperate to get in.

When they were done, the three boys, with Dottie at their feet, found themselves standing in front of a rusty iron gate.

Jack peered in through the bars, but it was almost impossible to see anything. Then suddenly Dottie shot through.

'Dottie, wait!' gasped Bruno, but she had disappeared into the darkness ahead.

'Well, we'll have to go now,' said Jack. He felt for a latch on the old rusty gate and couldn't find one. Then he simply nudged it forward and to his surprise it swung all the way open with a loud creak.

Bruno and Rocco jumped back instinctively.

'What if it is haunted … ?' Rocco whispered. He looked absolutely terrified.

'Ghosts can't hurt you,' Bruno said to him. 'They can't even touch you, remember? Their hands go right through you …'

'Yeah but what if it *throws* things at you like one of those poltergeists?'

'You can't throw something if you can't touch it …' said Bruno.

But Jack had stopped listening to the bickering brothers. He was completely focused on what lay in front of them. For beyond the gate was a path – in fact, Jack soon realised, a *tunnel* of unknowable blackness. Here the ivy seemed to have grown up out of the ground and over and down again on the other side, forming a sort of archway.

Jack took a tentative step forward. At once, tiny little tingles of excitement started running up the skin of his neck. What was at the end of this tunnel he hadn't a clue, but a sense of adventure swelled inside him, and as though being pulled by some mighty magnet, he began slowly moving further into it.

With one hand reaching out blindly in front of him, Jack walked forward until suddenly the tips of his fingers touched something. A hard wooden surface.

A door.

With a shiver of excitement, he ran his hand down it, feeling for a handle, but there didn't seem to be one.

Then, as with the gate, Jack pushed, and then pushed again a little harder, and the door swung calmly open. A soft light from somewhere within illuminated the narrow staircase that led upwards from the doorway, and as Jack's eyes adjusted his jaw dropped in disbelief.

What he saw was extraordinary.

For what was in front of him was just the same as what was behind him – a deep and endless forest of ivy, except this one was *inside the house*.

It was everywhere you looked. There was ivy running up the walls of the stairway, and across the ceiling. And as he entered the huge reception room at the top of the stairs, he saw what must have once been furniture – a side table, a hallway cabinet, perhaps an armchair – all bound tightly in green leaves. Any remnants of the household that once was had now been swallowed up by this unforgettable wilderness.

Jack could hear Bruno and Rocco at the base of the stairs now, debating whether or not to go in, but Jack's feet kept moving on of their own accord. He had never seen anything like this – a secret garden, a wild-dark forest, all set within the four walls of a house. Part of him felt uneasy and perhaps a little frightened. It all seemed so strange and unreal and so entirely removed from the world that he knew. But it also felt thrilling – as though he had discovered something totally untouched and completely hidden away from the rest of the world.

As he moved through the reception room towards

another winding staircase, he placed his hand softly against the leaves. They felt smooth and dry. He smiled and looked up the stairs in wonder. He had never seen anything so magnificent.

He mounted the stairway that swept its way up to the floor above as if hypnotised by the beauty around him. Looking down to his feet, he noticed that each step was carpeted with soft green moss and tiny yellow buttercups.

The stairs led up into a dimly lit room that seemed to be slanting to one side. The walls in this room were also covered in hanging ivy. In the corner of the room, however, there was something untouched by the vines. Something *new*, Jack realised with a shiver – a cooking pot resting over a small wood-burning stove.

Jack walked over to the steaming pot

and waved his nose
over it. It smelled like
hot milk.

But before he could
take in what this meant,
from out of nowhere, a
twisted vine hooked itself around Jack's
ankle. With a keen snap, the vine tripped
him up so that he fell on to his back on
the floor. But he had no time to cry out,
because a moment later, he felt himself
being whisked up into the air by his ankle,
so that he was hanging upside down. Then,
like a rocket, he flew towards the ceiling.

A blur of images whizzed past him as he
dizzied on upwards at an incredible speed.

Just as Jack thought to his horror that
he must be about to crash into the ceiling,
instead he shot clean through it, through
a large hole in the floor above, and on and

on higher and higher, as if he was
about to be launched through the
roof and fired out into the starry
sky. And then, suddenly, the vine's
upwards motion came to an abrupt
halt, jolting Jack sharply and leaving
him dangling there like a newly
caught fly.

Jack immediately began wriggling
and writhing, trying to free himself from
the vine's grip. But it was no use. It had
him in its grip, like the rest of the things
in the house. He hung there helplessly, still
swaying back and forth. Until, very slowly,
the motion came to stop and the world
around him became still.

A blurry image came into focus.
Someone or something was coming
towards him.

Now if this had been a web and Jack
the fly, then the spider was now looking

directly into his eyes. Only it wasn't a spider at all.

It was a girl.

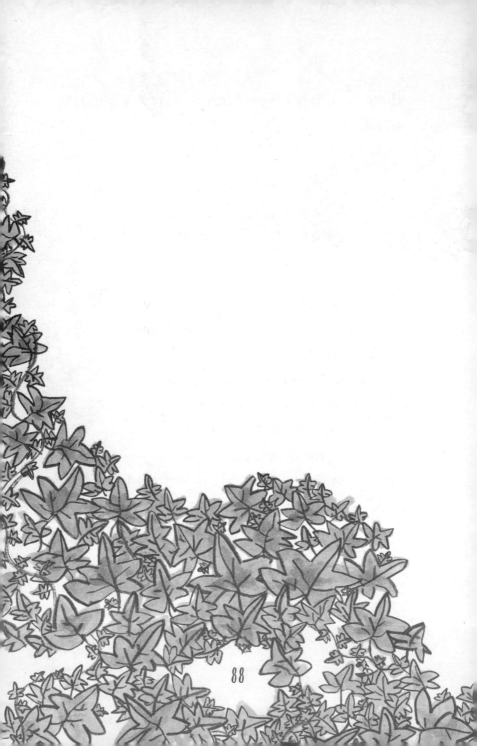

GIRL

Two large eyes the colour of glassy emeralds were staring into Jack's own.

A cry of terror rose up Jack's throat but before it could escape, a tiny hand slapped itself over his mouth.

And so they remained for a moment, eye to eye, hand over mouth, Jack still dangling upside down like a puppet on a string. Along with the green eyes, Jack could now see that the girl had a giant bird's nest of bright orange hair and little freckles dotted all over her pale skin. He had to admit, she didn't look that scary.

'Promise not to scream?' she said, narrowing her eyes at him.

Jack nodded, and the girl slowly took her hand away from his mouth.

'W-who are you?' Jack stammered. 'What is this place?'

The girl frowned at him and cocked her head to one side.

'Why should I tell you? Don't you know that this is a secret camp?' said the girl.

There was a giant gap between her two front teeth as if a bowling ball had smashed through them.

'Only exclusive members are allowed in here,' she said, 'and seeing as I'm the only member, that makes *you* an intruder! What are you? Some kind of thief?'

Jack was staring at the girl with
a look of perfect confusion.

'Speak, trespasser!' she snapped,
grabbing him by the collar and pulling
him close so their noses touched.

'I-I'm just a kid ...' Jack said nervously.

'A kid?' she responded suspiciously.
'Well, you look like the kind of kid I'd eat
for breakfast. Hey, speaking of which,
I'm hungry!'

She tugged at the vine that was
wrapped around Jack's ankle.
Immediately, it loosened its
grip, and Jack fell a
metre or so to the
ground.

'Hey!' he
shouted angrily,
rubbing his behind. He
was just stumbling to his
feet when the girl grabbed the hanging

vine and with a *SWOOSH* plummeted
back down through the hole in the floor.
Jack rushed over to the hole, peering
downwards. On the floor below, he could
see the girl standing smugly next to her
cooking pot, grinning up at him.

'Don't you have stairs to this floor?'
asked Jack. How on earth was he supposed
to get down?

'Come on!' cried the girl. 'Don't be
boring!'

'How do I do it!?' Jack shouted.

'Just do what I did!' she said simply.
'Grab the vine, and it will all become clear.'

Jack closed his eyes as tightly as he
could, gripped hold of the vine and then –
SWOOSH – down he went after her.

He went shooting down tremendously
fast and, in a flash, his body hit the
floor and went tumbling across it.
Feeling a little sick, Jack sat

up, shaking the dizziness out of his head. He looked around for the girl, but she seemed to have disappeared.

'Fun?' came a voice from somewhere above him.

Jack looked up to see the girl perched on another hanging loop of ivy, swaying back and forth on it, as if it were a swing.

Jack rubbed his eyes and gazed around the room in a daze. In the opposite corner to the bubbling pot of hot milk he saw a tent-like structure made from different coloured sheets, the top of which was held up by another vine that looped down from the ceiling. Towers of dusty books weighed down the wrinkled tent corners and a pointy grey feather was poking out of the top, like a flag.

The girl was watching him closely from her makeshift swing. Now that Jack wasn't hanging upside down, he was able to take her in properly for the first time.

Looking at her, Jack felt that she'd been abandoned by all humankind. Her face was smudgy with dirt and her clothes were scruffy, and several sizes too big.

'Sorry,' Jack said politely, 'but who are you?'

'I don't know really,' said the girl.

'Well, what's your name?'

The girl thought harder this time with one eye shut tight. 'I don't have one of those.'

'You don't have a name?' asked Jack. 'But surely you must have a name? Everybody has one.'

'I've never been able to remember mine,' she said casually. 'Dead annoying, really.'

Jack had never met anyone who couldn't

remember their name before. 'Where are your parents?' he asked her.

'Parents …' she mumbled quietly to herself as if she had simply misplaced them somewhere. 'Nope! Don't have any of those either. Wait! No, I have a dad! Somewhere. I think.'

And then, just as Jack's nerves were beginning to settle a little, the girl leapt off the swing and landed with a thud right in front of him. She leaned forward, staring into his eyes.

'You haven't seen him, have you?'

'No,' Jack said with wide eyes. 'I don't even know what he looks like.'

'Hmm,' the girl said thoughtfully. 'I know he's around here somewhere. I just haven't found him yet.'

A faint rustling of leaves suddenly caught Jack's attention. The girl spun around instantly and thrust her fists out as if ready for a duel.

She glared at the staircase that Jack had climbed up minutes earlier, and stepped in front of Jack, as if to protect him.

'Don't worry, I think I know who it is,' said Jack as two figures appeared. It was Bruno and Rocco.

The brothers stopped dead at the top of the stairs, and remained there, looking between Jack and the girl suspiciously. Jack couldn't help smiling. He could tell they had no idea what to make of this curious girl, with her crazy hair and her funny clothes. They watched her as if they had stumbled upon a newly discovered species.

'These are my friends, Bruno and Rocco,' said Jack to

the girl.

Bruno and Rocco mumbled a hello.

'And this is …' He looked at the girl, who just shrugged. 'She doesn't remember.'

'She doesn't remember what?' asked Rocco.

'Her name,' said Jack. Bruno's and Rocco's faces creased into expressions of confusion. But before they could quiz her, Dottie came tearing up the stairs and into the room.

'There you are, Dottie!' said Bruno, giving her a pat as she bounded towards first him, then Rocco, and then Jack, who gave her a satisfying scratch beneath her chin.

'What creature is this?' whispered the girl curiously, her eyes growing wide.

The three boys looked at each other.

'Er, it's a dog?' Rocco said, frowning.

'Oh, fantastic!' the girl cried. 'I've

read about these. They're
supposed to be really friendly,
aren't they?'

'You've never met a dog before?'
Bruno asked suspiciously.

'I don't *think* so,' the girl said. 'Not that
I can remember anyway.'

The girl cocked her head to one side.
'Do dogs like milk?' she asked.

'Yeah, they love it!' Rocco said. 'Dogs
are like me. They pretty much eat
anything.'

'I love milk too!' said the girl as she
went over to her pot and spooned some
into a little dish, setting it on the ground
for Dottie, who lapped it up in seconds.
'I make a pot of milk every evening for
breakfast. It sets me up perfectly for the
night.'

The boys exchanged another look.

'Sorry,' Jack said, 'but don't you mean

you have it for breakfast *in the morning*?'

'Breakfast in the morning!' the girl said, laughing, as if this was a great joke. 'I can't eat breakfast in the morning. Morning's when I go to sleep.'

The boys were staring at her with baffled expressions on their faces.

'So let me get this straight,' said Bruno, eyeing the girl suspiciously. 'You stay up all night and sleep during the day?'

'Of course!' said the girl. 'Don't you do that?'

Jack looked at her for any hint that she was making fun of them, but she seemed perfectly genuine.

'No, that's daft!' said Rocco.

'We do it the other way round,' Jack added more gently. 'We sleep at night-time and are awake during the day.'

Rocco yawned and began rubbing his eyes. It was very late and all the excitement was beginning to make them feel tired.

The girl watched him, unimpressed.

'I'm sorry, but I'm not sure you lot are going to have what it takes to be in this gang,' she said firmly.

'Gang?' said Bruno. 'What gang?'

'*My* gang,' the girl said. 'It's a secret gang, just for detectives. I can't have you lot around being all sleepy and dragging your feet, you know.'

The girl was now pacing back and forth in front of them, her arms behind her back, like a general preparing her soldiers for a great battle.

'I need you as fit as fiddles if I'm ever going to solve the mystery.'

'What mystery?' said Bruno.

The girl looked up at him, her face suddenly blank. Then she looked at Jack, as if for help.

'Um,' said Jack, 'is it the mystery of where your dad is?'

'*Yes!*' said the girl.

'And what your name is?' asked Rocco.

'Oh yes, that too!' cried the girl happily.

'Er, aren't we forgetting the *main* mystery here?' said Bruno. 'Have you looked around this place recently?'

The girl cast her eyes wonderingly around the room, as if seeing it for the first time. 'It is a *bit* odd, isn't it?' she said. 'Well, in that case, you can see why I need to solve all these mysteries,' she went on, getting some of her fighting tone back. 'I need to work out who I am and where my dad is so we can go home together,' she said.

'So this isn't your home?' asked Jack.

'I don't know,' said the girl with a shrug.

'It might be.'

For a moment, Jack thought she seemed a little sad, but then she straightened up and looked each of them in the eye in turn and said, 'So anyway, you can only join the gang if you help me. Is that clear?'

'Of course we'll help you,' said Jack simply. 'Won't we?' He looked over at Rocco and Bruno.

Rocco nodded his head seriously without saying a word. Bruno, however, said nothing. He stared back at the girl.

'We'll help you if you can look after Dottie,' he said firmly.

The girl stared into Bruno's eyes. She looked thoughtful for a second, tapping her bottom lip with her finger. Then she nodded at him to go on.

'My aunt's been horrible to her,' Bruno said, scuffing his feet on the floor. 'She kept her tied to a tree outside with no food or water, and she won't let her in the house. So she's been all alone out there. If we promise to help you solve your mystery, then you need to promise to keep Dottie safe. Just for a couple of days, and then we'll take her home.'

Bruno didn't look up at the girl until he'd finished, so it was only then that he saw the girl's eyes had begun to glisten with tears.

But Jack had been watching her the whole time. He was completely fascinated, watching her try to control the emotions on her face.

'Dottie will be safe here,' she said gruffly, brushing away a tear. 'No one should have to be alone. She can stay as long as she wants.'

Jack was touched by the girl's words. She must relate to Dottie, he thought, being all alone herself. Jack knew how that felt too.

He could see the Buckleys were touched by her words as well. It wasn't often, after all, that they got to experience an act of simple kindness from a perfect stranger.

'Thanks,' said Rocco quietly. Jack didn't think he'd ever seen him be so polite.

'You hear that, Dottie?' Bruno called to her, mussing her fur roughly when she came padding over. 'You don't have to sleep outside any more. You'll be safe when the storm comes.'

A strange, distant look came over the girl's face. 'When the storm comes ...' she whispered, as if deep in thought.

'Um, yup,' said Jack. 'Apparently there's a—'

'When the storm comes!' she repeated again, looking up at them with widening eyes. 'That's when my dad left! When the storm came!'

Then, very slowly, she pulled out a tiny

piece of folded paper from her pocket. The paper was so thin and delicate, Jack was sure that even blowing on it would make it crumble away like burning paper in a fire.

She opened the note and the boys huddled behind her, looking over her shoulder. She held it out gently in front of them, so they could all read it.

Jack could feel his heart beating faster now.

The writing was small and messy and all the letters were slanting to one side. The girl read it out loud:

When the next storm comes,

I'll be gone ... will come back

and tell you everything!

Love Dad

'Wow!' said Bruno. 'Where do you think he went? Is he scared of storms?'

'Dottie's scared of storms,' said Rocco.

'Yeah but she's a *dog*, you idiot.'

The girl gave a small smile as she carefully folded up the note again and pushed it back into her pocket. But Jack could see that the smile didn't make it to her eyes.

'Maybe if he disappeared during that storm, he'll come back during this one?' said Jack, trying to sound as positive as he could.

'This is definitely our first clue anyway!' said Rocco, backing up Jack. 'And it's a really good one.'

The girl looked at Rocco. 'So it is!' She looked much cheerier again, and with a sudden burst of energy, she leapt up on to a small wooden chest. She stood proudly upright, placed her hand over her heart and closed her eyes.

'I hereby pledge allegiance to Dottie the dog, and promise to keep her safe along with all the other animals of the world.'

One of her eyes popped open, and it glared at the boys.

The boys looked a bit embarrassed, but they all followed suit, placing their hands on to their chests and mumbling, 'And we

promise to help you find your dad …'

'And remember your name!' added Rocco.

'And remember what time of day breakfast is,' mumbled Bruno under his breath.

'Great!' the girl cheered as she leapt down from the chest. 'You're in! Welcome to the secret summer gang! We just need something to seal the deal …'

She looked thoughtful for a moment, before producing a small penknife from her pocket. She flipped it open. The boys looked at each other anxiously. Then they watched in wide-eyed disbelief as the girl sliced off three locks of fuzzy hair from her head, and placed one solemnly in each of their hands.

'Er, thanks?' said Bruno, while he and Rocco seemed barely able to contain their giggles.

Jack looked down at the strange offering in his hands and wondered if this was the kind of gift you had to keep or you could just throw away.

'First official meeting tomorrow morning!' she said.

'Morning as in … the beginning of the day?' Jack asked, thinking it best to be sure.

'Yes, and we can have a morning breakfast too,' said the girl, 'then maybe you won't all be so tired and pathetic!'

'Morning breakfast it is,' Jack said with a smile.

'But won't you be asleep at that time?' Rocco said.

'No way!' said the girl, bending down to give Dottie a firm pat. 'I've got a dog to take care of now.'

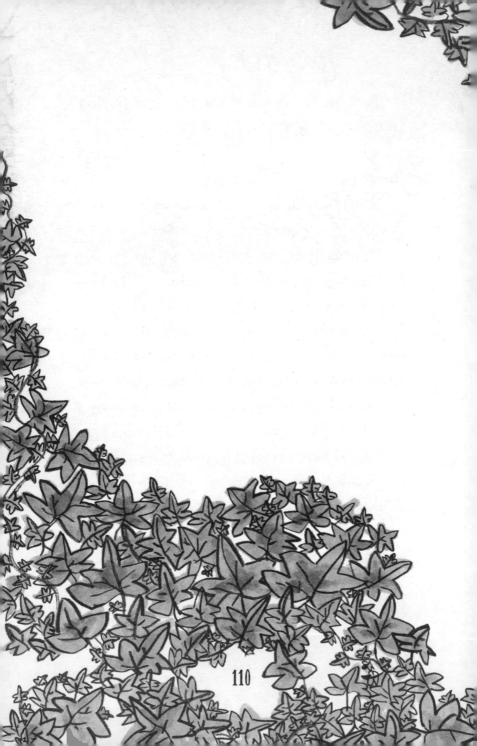

110

THE GLASS BOTTLE

Jack was in a daze as he walked back down the moss-covered stairs, through the ivy tunnel and back out into the night. He was so taken aback by the whole thing, he could hardly believe what had just happened.

'She's quite tricky, isn't she,' Bruno said as he and Rocco stumbled out behind Jack.

'What do you mean, *tricky*?' asked Rocco.

'I mean, she's not exactly normal, is she,' he said, rubbing his sleepy eyes. 'I wouldn't want to go on a picnic with her, let's just say that.'

'Well, maybe she wouldn't want to go on a picnic with *you*,' Rocco cried. 'I know I wouldn't.' Then after a moment he added more quietly, 'I think she's nice.'

'She is looking after Dottie for you …' said Jack. He liked the girl too, though he had to admit, she wasn't the usual sort of person you met every day. She had something about her, something strange and almost … magical.

The time was two o'clock in the morning and Jack knew he should be feeling exhausted as it was way past his bedtime. But as the Buckleys waved him goodnight and he slipped back through his garden gate and across the moonlit lawn, he felt more awake than he ever had. Who *was* this strange girl and what could have happened to her to make her forget even her own name?

As Jack reached the back door, he noticed that all the lights in his house were still off. He breathed a sigh of relief and opened the door as quietly as he could, then deposited his shoes and coat in the hall and crept upstairs.

As soon as he saw his bed, he flopped face first on to it. It felt great to lie down – maybe he was a little tired after all.

It had been an incredible night and the secret summer gang had been formed. Only two days ago Jack had felt completely alone in the world, and now he was part of a gang! He had always dreamed of being in a gang. Not only that, but Dottie was safe, and as that comforting thought took hold, Jack fell into a deep, dreamless sleep.

Jack woke to the sound of Ozzie meowing incessantly for his breakfast, right in his ear. Ozzie was practically sitting on Jack's head and was scraping his furry chin against the tip of Jack's nose.

Jack sighed and looked over at the clock. It was still early, and Jack hadn't had nearly enough sleep, but there was no time for a lie-in. Jack had a meeting to attend! He leapt out of bed, suddenly wide awake, and dressed as quickly as he could. He carried Ozzie downstairs, poured some food into his bowl and hurried on over to the empty house.

It was the most marvellous thing to be heading there again. Jack had been curious about the place for so many years, and now it was the headquarters of their secret gang! Well, that made him feel like the luckiest kid there ever was.

As he made his way across his back garden, a voice in Jack's head couldn't help but wonder, *Did I dream it all?* But as Jack opened

the rusty gate and entered the strange ivy
tunnel, he knew for sure it was all true.

When he got to the wooden door, he
found it open. The ivy-lined stairway
looked just as mysterious and magical as
it had the night before, as did the strange
reception room, with its ghostly evergreen
furniture. Now that it was daytime, Jack
could also see that there were rooms to
either side of the moss-covered stairway.
The doors were all teasingly ajar, and Jack
couldn't resist having a peek inside.

He tiptoed slowly over to the rooms on
the left of the staircase and peered in …
Inside one was a huge four-poster bed, ivy
curled around its four pillars, and to either
side of the bedroom were a little kitchen
and a bathroom, both entirely consumed
by the twisting ivy, so that cupboards and
cookers and toilets and baths were almost
unrecognisable. Jack was just walking over

to check out the room to the right of the staircase when Dottie pushed her way through the door.

'What were you doing in there, girl?' asked Jack, as Dottie curled her way around his leg. She gave him a quick lick on the hand and then went straight back through the same door.

Jack was about to follow her in when he realised he could hear voices coming from upstairs.

As Jack walked up the mossy stairs, he was surprised to see the Buckleys were already there.

'Is that where you sleep then?' Rocco was asking.

'Yeah, I love tents!' the girl said. 'They're warmer than just being in a normal bed and much more fun to build. Do you want to see? Hey, kid!' she said, waving as she caught sight of Jack. 'Come and join us …'

The girl was lifting the entrance flap
of the tent to show the Buckleys what
was inside. Jack came over to join them,
crouching down and peering over Rocco's
shoulder.

'Wicked!' said Rocco. 'I wish *my*
bed was like that.'

Jack had to admit, it did look
cosy. There was a huge mound of fluffy
covers and soft pillows of all different
colours and materials. It looked like the
most comfortable bed in the world.

'Hey!' Bruno suddenly cried. 'Those are
my space covers!'

He pushed right past the girl, who was
backing away from the tent a little shiftily,
Jack thought. When Bruno came out again
he was clutching his duvet cover. It was
covered in planets and glowing green stars.

'It was *you*!' he cried at the girl. 'You're
the one who stole my space covers!'

'I only *borrowed* them,' said the girl rather mischievously. 'I was going to put them back.'

'Yeah right,' Bruno snapped.

'Hey!' Rocco shouted at his brother. 'You said I'd stolen them! I told you I didn't, and you didn't believe me. Say you're sorry!'

'I'm not saying sorry!' Bruno pointed at the girl. '*She* should be the one saying sorry! Those are my best covers ever! They glow in the dark!'

'I know, they're fantastic!' the girl cried. 'You can have them back now. I only wanted them for a bit.'

'How did you get them, anyway?' asked Bruno.

'They were on the washing line one night, and I could see them glowing there … they looked so lovely,' she said, her shoulders drooping. 'I'm sorry. You can take them back now.'

'I will, thank you very much!' shouted Bruno. He looked as if he was about to make off down the stairs with them when something fell out of the covers and hit the ground.

It was a small glass bottle. It didn't break, but rolled across the floorboards and kept rolling, eventually stopping at Jack's feet.

Jack knelt down and picked it up. The bottle was made of dark glass and was very small with a tiny label sellotaped on to it. It looked like something you'd find inside the wreckage of an old ship buried beneath the sea.

'What is it?' Jack asked, as the others gathered round.

'I don't know,' she said. 'I found it in the house.'

Jack looked at it closely. There was

nothing inside the little bottle as far as
Jack could see, but there seemed to be
something written on the label.

'What does it say?' Bruno asked,
dropping the covers on the floor.

It was hard to read as the ink had almost
completely faded away. The handwriting
was also tiny and wildly slanted.

With squinted eyes, Jack read it
out slowly.

*Blossom at the
bakery. Age nine.*

'It's the same handwriting as the note …' said Jack, thinking hard. He turned to the girl. 'You're about nine, aren't you?' he asked.

'I suppose so,' she said.

'Do you think Blossom might be your name?'

'Yes!' she said, leaping in the air. 'Yes, I think it is! Hey, call me Blossom, everyone!'

Rocco began to jump around too. 'You have a name! You have a name! We've solved the first mystery!' And he and Blossom danced around the room together.

'So what's the bakery bit about?' said Bruno, who was still a bit grumpy about the covers.

Blossom sighed and said nothing for a few seconds as though she was searching for something to say.

'I have trouble remembering things,' she

121

said quietly. 'I remember the bakery … and eating cake. The cake was delicious! The most delicious I've ever had. And my dad was there smiling down at me, and the sun was shining … It was a perfect moment. That was the last time I saw Dad, I think. Then after that I don't remember much, except finding myself here.'

Jack was hanging on her every word. 'But is this your home?'

'I don't know,' said Blossom. 'It feels familiar …'

'But your dad wasn't here?'

'I searched the whole house,' Blossom continued. 'Funny thing is, I can't even remember what Dad looks like now …'

The boys remained silent.

'Can you remember anything about him?' Jack asked her.

'I'm not sure,' she said, trying hard to think. 'Sometimes I think I can, but it's all a bit blurry. It comes and then it goes again.'

'It's OK,' said Jack. 'My mum disappeared a while ago, and I don't remember what she looks like either.'

Blossom glanced up at Jack and a brief look of understanding was shared between them.

'So … about the bottle,' said Bruno, clearly trying to move things on a bit.

'Yes,' said Jack, 'where did you find it?'

Blossom's face suddenly took on that distant look again. Her eyes were staring unblinkingly at nothing, as if she was deep in thought.

There was a tense silence that seemed to go on for ever.

Then without warning Blossom leapt in the air and exclaimed, 'Aha!' She looked at Jack, her bright green eyes sparkling with an expression of excitement that slowly spread across her face.

'I remember where I found it!' she cried.
'Come with me! I'll show you …'

ANIMAL LIST

Blossom raced off into the far corner
of the room behind the tent and the boys
quickly followed.

Jack saw there was another huge hole
in the floor here, like the one he'd been
dragged up through the day before. He
realised this must be above the room that
Dottie had come out of earlier.

'This way!' Blossom called back to the
boys. Just as she had done last time, she
leapt on to a hanging vine and then –
SWOOSH! – down she shot.

Bruno's and Rocco's mouths fell open as

they stood over the hole.

'H-how did she do that?' stammered Rocco.

'Did she slide down it?' asked Bruno, frowning. 'Or did the vine … er, it looked as if it …' He scratched his head, unsure how to finish the sentence.

'Try not to think about it too much!' called out Blossom brightly. 'Just jump!'

'It's actually easier than it looks,' said Jack. He leapt at the vine and zoomed down it to join Blossom on the floor below.

Bruno and Rocco looked at each other, then at the same moment, they both pounced on the vine.

'Wooooooohoooo!' they screamed as they both went whizzing down it together.

'That was FUN!' shouted Rocco. 'Can we do it again?'

But Jack wasn't listening. He was staring round at the room in wonder. The ivy seemed to grow particularly thickly in this room. The whole of the back wall was covered with ivy so thick that you couldn't even catch a glimpse of the bricks behind it. The ivy was like a curtain, heavy and impenetrable.

And sniffing about at the base of the curtain was Dottie.

'She loves it in here,' said Blossom. 'She was sniffing around there all night long. I even felt behind the ivy to see if there was anything there, but it's just a wall.'

'What *is* this room?' asked Jack.

'This is where I found the bottles,' said Blossom. 'They were all over the floor, where the holes are.'

'Bottle*s*?' said Bruno. 'So there are more than one?'

'Oh yes!' said Blossom.

'They were everywhere!'

Jack now noticed that the floorboards were dotted with holes, and wherever there was a hole, a number of vines had shot up through it, snaked across the floor, and joined the great curtain of ivy on the back wall.

'That must be how the vines got in,' Jack muttered to himself. 'This is where it started …'

He crouched down to inspect one of the holes.

Surrounding it there seemed to be some sort of hardened liquid. It looked as if the liquid had seeped through the floorboards and into the soil underneath the house. Jack knelt down to check out the other holes and found they were all the same.

'I wonder what made the holes?' Jack said quietly.

'Maybe whatever was in the bottles?'

Blossom said.

'So where are they?' asked Bruno.

'Where are what?' said Blossom.

'The bottles!'

Before she could answer, there was a yelp from behind them.

It was Rocco. He seemed to be wrestling with a vine from the curtain.

'Is the ivy, um, alive …?' Rocco asked with a shaky voice.

'Of course it's alive,' said Bruno grumpily. 'I mean, all plants are alive, aren't they?

'Yes, but … I think it just tapped me on the shoulder …'

'Don't be ridiculous,' said Bruno. But he didn't sound too sure.

Jack turned to Blossom. '*Is* the ivy

magical?' he asked her.

'It might be magical, I suppose …' she said, with a slight twinkle in her eye, 'but I can't really remember.'

'This room gives me the creeps,' said Rocco. 'Can we go back upstairs?'

'I have an idea!' said Blossom.

'Let's all have some nice warm milk! I always find that helps.'

And without waiting for anyone's reply, she went over to the thick vine they had all slid down, gave it a firm tug, and a moment later she shot back up through the hole to the floor above.

'Is this a dream?' said Bruno. He was

standing there blinking up at the hole in a daze.

'Well, if it is,' Jack said quietly, 'we're all having the same one.'

'I guess that answers the question of whether the ivy's magical anyway,' said Rocco.

'Come on!' shouted Blossom, her freckled face peering down at them through the hole. 'I have to show you the other bottles ... I remember where they are now!'

Once they'd all got over the strange experience of being pulled up through the ceiling by a vine, the boys decided maybe some warm milk might not be a bad idea. They plonked themselves down on the floor by the tent, while Blossom prepared the milk on her stove.

'Whose are all these books?' asked

Bruno, gazing at the towers of books
around her tent.

'My dad's, I guess,' Blossom said, stirring
the pot of milk.

'I don't like books,' Rocco said. 'Too
many words.'

'You can't read, anyway!' Bruno scoffed
at him.

'Yes, I can!' Rocco snapped back. 'I just
prefer comics. I like the pictures.'

'My favourite book has pictures too,'
said Blossom, bringing over one large mug
and a bowl of steaming milk. 'You'll have to
share, I'm afraid. These are all I have.'

'Thanks,' said Jack, savouring the warm
comforting smell as he took a swig and
passed it on.

'What's your favourite book?' Rocco
asked Blossom.

'I found it in the room downstairs. I
keep it in the chest with my other

special things …'

Blossom suddenly leapt across the floor and without warning pushed Bruno off the wooden chest where he was sitting.

'Hey!' Bruno yelled, landing in an awkward heap on the floor.

'Sorry, but you're sitting on my special chest!' Blossom carefully lifted the lid, and from inside pulled out a large book. She dropped it on to the floor with a heavy *THUD*.

'This is a very precious book,' she said, as the rest of them huddled round. 'It's my animal encyclopaedia,' she added proudly. 'It has every animal in the world inside.'

Blossom began flicking through the pages

and arrived at a picture of a large grey elephant.

'This is my favourite creature in the whole animal kingdom. When I get big, I'm going to have a whole family of them and we'll go exploring together. The big ones will carry me on their backs and I'll teach the baby ones how to roll around in the mud.'

Her eyes were sparkling with wonder as she touched the picture with the tip of her finger.

'My dad works at the animal home,' said Jack. 'There's an elephant there. Maybe we can go and see it one day?'

Blossom's eyes became as wide as headlamps. 'Really? What's an animal home, anyway?'

'It's like a zoo but all the animals there are old. They can't really look after themselves any more.'

'That sounds like the best job in the world,' she said with a sigh.

'So, um, are the bottles in the chest too?' asked Jack. He didn't want to be pushy, but she seemed to have completely forgotten what they were actually looking for.

'Oh yes!' she said. 'Let me show you.'

She passed the animal encyclopaedia over to Rocco, and reached into her chest again. Inside were a series of bottles, each one exactly like the first one they had found inside Bruno's covers – made of thick, dark glass, with a small white label on the front.

Jack and Bruno each picked one up and the read the label.

'Two hundred and seventeen,' Jack read.

'This one says six,' said Bruno.

'Yes, they've all got numbers on them,' said Blossom brightly.

'Well, that doesn't help us much,' said Jack, feeling bitterly disappointed. He had been so sure the bottles would hold the answer to finding Blossom's dad somehow.

'Hey!' shouted Rocco suddenly.

'What is it?' asked Bruno.

'This just fell out of the book …' said Rocco, passing a piece of paper to Blossom.

It was notepaper, and on it was written a list of animals – in the same slanting handwriting that was on the bottles and the note from Blossom's dad.

Cheetah – for speed (can reach
68 miles per hour in
3 seconds)

Tortoise – for long life (200+ years)

Falcon – for flying

Shark – for breathing in water

Horse – for hearing

'Look!' Blossom said, pointing excitedly to the last animal on the list.

Jack leaned in closer and read it aloud: '*Elephant – for remembering.*'

There was another paragraph of writing beneath this. It said:

I think it is perhaps the elephant which is the most powerful of all creatures as its memory is immeasurably superior to all other species. Elephants are constantly reminiscing and telling stories which I very much enjoy listening to. They remember everything.

'What does he mean, *telling stories?*' scoffed Bruno. 'Elephants can't tell stories!'

'How do you know?' said Rocco. 'They probably do – we just can't understand them!'

'I don't know what it means,' said Jack,

looking up at Blossom. 'But if this is your dad's book, then it looks as if elephants are your dad's favourite animal too.'

Then Bruno noticed something else on the list. 'Look, there's a page number next to the note about the elephant – page one hundred and nineteen,' he said, grabbing the book from Rocco.

'Hey!' said Rocco, crossing his arms in a grump as Bruno began flicking through the pages. When he got to page 119 he gasped. 'It's the elephant!'

An idea suddenly struck Jack. 'You found this book in the room with the bottles, right?' he asked Blossom.

'Yes,' she said.

'Then maybe the numbers on the bottles refer to page numbers too?'

Blossom's eyes lit up. She grabbed one

of the bottles and read out the number on it. 'Eighty-one!'

Bruno immediately began flicking through the book again till he got to page 81. 'The tortoise!'

'That's on the list too!' said Bruno. 'Try another ...'

Blossom turned back to the chest and found Rocco was already pulling out one of the bottles.

'Hey!' she said, trying to grab it back from him. But he was too fast.

'This one's got a cork in it!' cried Rocco. He uncorked it, and a small brightly coloured ball poured out into his hand.

'Ooh, a gobstopper!' he said. And before anyone could stop him, he popped it in his mouth.

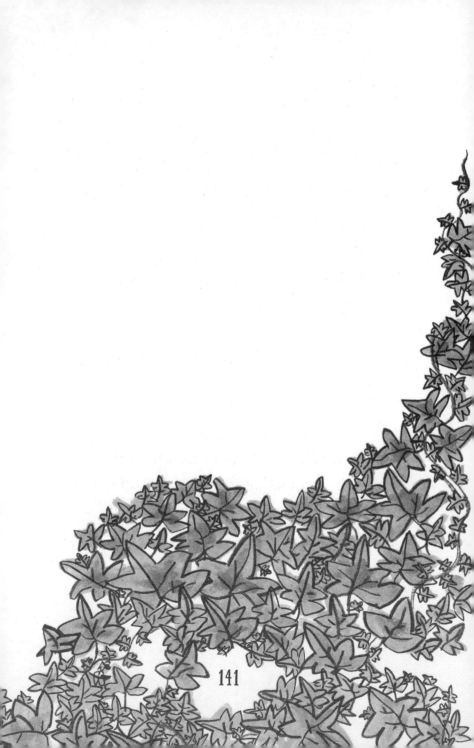

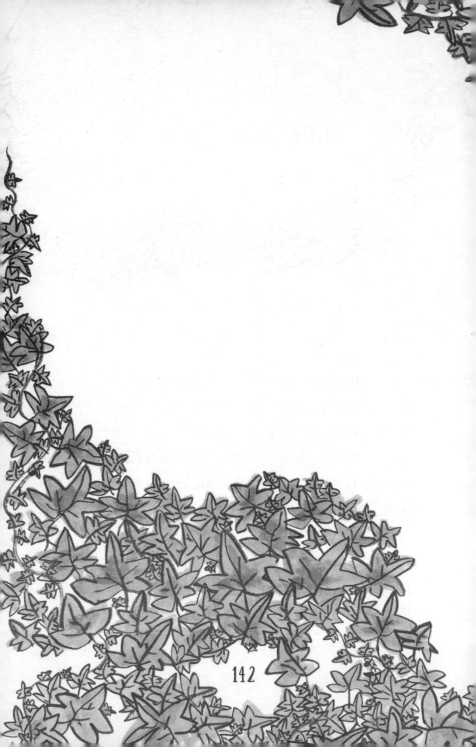
142

GOBSTOPPERS!

'Rocco, no!' shouted Jack. But it was too late.

Blossom's eyes grew wide.

'What have you eaten?' Bruno said, like a cross parent does when their child is hiding something from them.

'Nothing,' Rocco mumbled with his mouth full. 'It's none of your business anyway. It's mine. I found it.'

Bruno could barely make out what his brother was saying. There was something the size of a ping-pong ball wedged firmly inside his cheek.

'Spit it out!' Bruno demanded, holding his hand out beneath Rocco's chin.

Rocco shook his head at him.

Within a split second, Bruno had dived over and snatched the bottle from Rocco's grip. He looked inside but it was empty now.

'It's just a gobstopper!' Rocco grumbled.

'Rocco, those aren't gobstoppers!' said Jack. 'We don't know *what* they are!'

'I swallowed it!' Rocco gasped, with a look of dread in his eyes.

'You idiot!' said Bruno.

At first it didn't seem as though anything was going to happen. Then Rocco's hips suddenly jerked outwards as if he'd been given an electric shock. He immediately clutched his arms around his tummy and started giggling. Within seconds he was

wiggling and jiggling
about all over the floor.
'It tickles!' Rocco was
spluttering. 'It's bursting!
It's bursting inside of me!'
Then he leapt up and began hopping
madly around the room.

The others were trying desperately not
to laugh at him, but they just couldn't stop
themselves. Rocco looked so hilarious. It
was like watching someone who had the
funniest itch in the world. He was bouncing
around like a deranged kangaroo and
everyone was now roaring with laughter.

'I can feel it rolling around in my belly!'
Rocco squealed. 'It tickles! It tickles! It's
making me all giggly!'

'Whoa!' shrieked Blossom suddenly.
She pointed to his feet, her eyes nearly
popping out of their sockets. 'Your feet

aren't touching the
ground!'

'What are you
talking about?' said
Rocco. He looked
down and gasped.
Because it was true –
he was hovering a few
centimetres off the ground.

'I'm floating!' he cried.

His whole body began twitching back
and forth as he awkwardly tried to
steady himself, balancing as if he were
standing on an invisible skateboard.

'I'm not controlling this!' Rocco
yelled out in a funny voice.

'Flap your arms!' shouted Blossom.

'Flap my arms?' Rocco retorted.

'Yes! Flap them like wings! Pretend
you're a bird!'

So Rocco flapped his arms. He

immediately went flying up towards the ceiling.

'What's happening?' he shouted. He looked so happy and so terrified all at once.

Jack couldn't believe his eyes. 'You're … you're flying!' he said.

Rocco seemed to quickly discover that if he flapped his right arm down hard, he ever so slightly banked to the right. And if he flapped his left arm down, he turned ever so slightly to the left.

'I can do it!' Rocco gasped. 'It's working! I can change direction!'

He went sweeping around the room just like a bird. He flew upwards and downwards and side to side.

'Are you OK up there?' Jack shouted.

'Of course I'm OK!' Rocco chuckled. 'I can fly! It's the most brilliant feeling ever!'

He whooped and laughed as he turned circles in the air. He looked so silly and jolly up there.

Jack was suddenly gripped by an idea. 'Blossom, where's the bottle he got it from?' he asked urgently. 'What does the label say?'

Blossom found the bottle. 'Two hundred and twenty-six!' she shouted out, and Jack quickly flicked through the pages of the book. He gasped as he got to page 226.

He held the page up for Blossom to see.

The Falcon

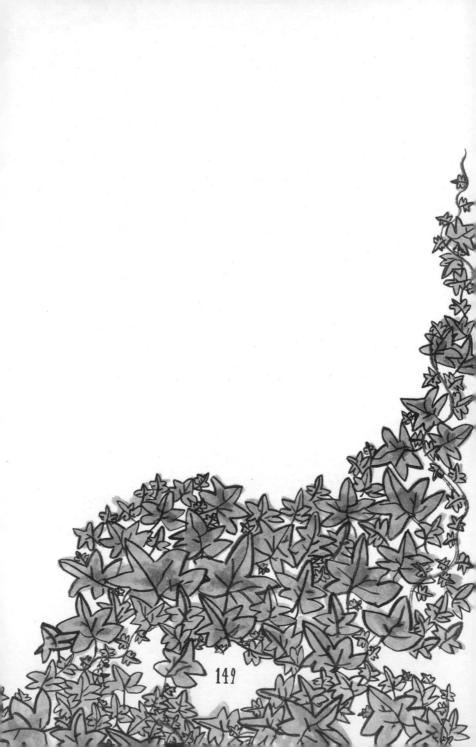

149

150

THE BUCKLEYS' POWERS

It was the biggest clue they'd had yet, and clearly proved what they'd known all along – there was magic in the house. Now they knew for sure that the magic had come from the bottles, and it seemed as if they knew the source of that magic too. Or at least, they knew that the magic was in some way related to the animals in the book.

While Rocco swooped and soared around the room like a bird, Jack, Blossom and Bruno went back over to the chest and started looking through the rest of the bottles.

'Try to find another one that's still got a cork in it!' said Jack.

'Here's one!' said Bruno, holding it up.

Jack and Blossom gathered round and they all stared at the small round object inside the bottle. It certainly could be mistaken for a gobstopper.

'Look!' cried Blossom. 'It's moving ...'

They peered at it more closely, and their mouths dropped open. Blossom was right. The gobstopper was hovering gently in the centre of the bottle without even touching the sides.

'How is it doing that?' Jack whispered.

'Let's take the cork out,' said Bruno, popping it off. The little round sphere bobbed out of the bottle and into his hand.

'Bruno, don't do anything stupid with that,' said Jack.

'Who, me?' said Bruno with a playful

grin, and before anyone
could stop him, he'd tossed the
gobstopper into his mouth.

'Bruno!' Jack shouted. But it was
too late.

Bruno grinned as he began rolling
the gobstopper in his mouth. His lips
and his cheeks were moving around at
the same time in different directions.

Blossom clapped her hands gleefully.
'This is such fun!' she cried. 'What's
going to happen this time?'

Jack checked the number on the
bottle – fifty-six – then turned to that
page in the book.

'The cheetah!' whispered Jack to
Blossom. 'That's on the animal list too!' He
looked at the list again to see what it said.
'It says, "Cheetah – for speed".'

Jack and Blossom were now staring at
Bruno intently. Nothing seemed to happen

for ages. And then, like Rocco, Bruno started laughing like a maniac.

'HAAAAHHHHHHHHAAAHAAAA!' he screamed, and then, as if by some miracle, he suddenly shot forward in a blur and disappeared out of the room!

'Where did he go?' cried Jack in shock.

There was a small tremble beneath their feet and a blurry shape came shooting back into the room, sending the open book flying, pages flapping.

'How are you doing that?' Jack said to Bruno, who was now standing next to him with his eyes as wide as two dinner plates.

'I have no idea!' Bruno panted. 'When I push down hard with my foot I just burst forward! Pretty cool, eh … ? Hey, Rocco!' he taunted. 'You're not the only Buckley with special powers!'

'Yeah, but can you do this?' said Rocco as he swooped down to fly at his brother, but by the time he'd got there Bruno was on the other side of the room.

'Haha!' said Bruno. 'Catch me if you can!'

Jack turned to Blossom and said, 'What is going on here?'

'I knew there was magic in this house!' she whispered excitedly.

'But where is it coming from? Do you think ...' Jack started, unsure of what exactly he was trying to say. 'Do you think your dad is somehow ... magical?'

'He must be!' said Blossom happily.

A wondrous and fantastical secret lay inside this house, that was clear now, and Jack longed to discover where this magic was coming from, and what it had to do with Blossom's strange situation and her missing dad.

It was at that moment that Jack heard a sound from outside – a tapping at the window. It was the rain. The storm must be coming. And what was more – it was nearly dinner time.

'Oh no …' said Jack. 'I have to go … before my dad gets back.'

Just then the sound of loud barking drifted up from downstairs. 'Dottie!' said Jack. 'Has she been in that room all this time?'

A moment later she came bounding up the stairs, running straight past Jack and Blossom and over to the corner of the room behind the tent, where the large hole was.

'What is it, girl?' asked Jack, and they followed her over there.

'Look!' Blossom cried.

Jack didn't know what she was talking about at first. Then he saw them – two floating spheres, like the gobstoppers. They were drifting up from the room below, through the hole … and they were coming towards Jack and Blossom.

They came to a stop,
floating weightlessly in the air just
above their heads.

'They're from him!' Blossom
whispered. 'He knows I'm here!'

'Who?' asked Rocco, confused.

'From Dad!' cried Blossom.

'How do you know?' asked Jack.

'I just know!' she said. 'It's a clue …
He's trying to help us find him!'

The magical balls were now swirling
around each other like glowing fireflies.

'Why are they moving like that?'
asked Bruno.

The gobstoppers were moving one way
then turning back on themselves and going
another, but they never touched. They
avoided bumping into one another like
people do on a busy street.

'It's because they're magic,' said

Blossom simply.

She reached her hand out delicately, taking one of the spheres in her palm. There was an orange light inside it that was glowing and pulsing.

She looked at Jack, and he knew she meant for him to do the same.

Jack slowly stepped towards the other sphere and took it in his hand. 'I wonder what these ones do?' he said.

Blossom grinned at him. 'Ready to find out?' she said.

Jack looked down at it. The sphere was such a beautiful thing to look at with its sparkling orange light beating like a heart in the palm of his hand.

He knew something crazy was about to happen but there was a part of him that wasn't afraid.

Blossom's twinkling green eyes watched Jack's face hopefully.

He nodded, and
they both popped them
into their mouths.

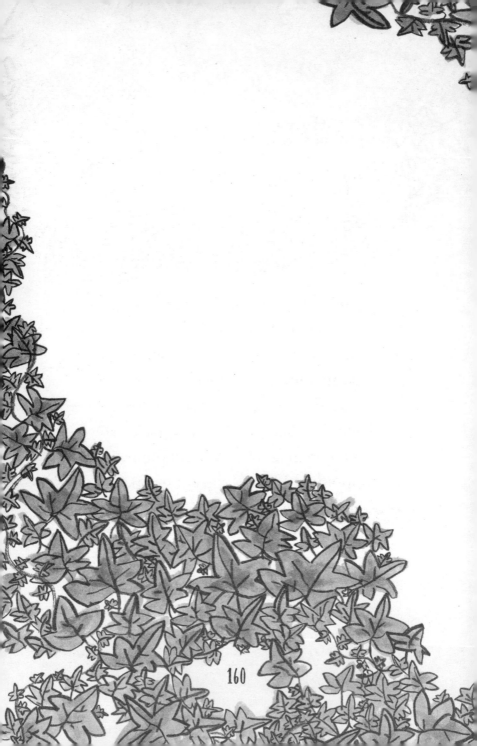

SWEET APRICOTS

The little ball of magic was surprisingly sweet-tasting and Jack could feel it shrinking in his mouth. Oncc it had melted away some more, he gulped it down and felt a hot tickle at the back of his throat.

Then, just like the Buckleys, Jack and Blossom began leaping around the room like hopping rabbits as the gobstoppers burst inside their tummies.

Jack was wriggling about as if there were a snake in his T-shirt, clinging to his stomach which was twitching and jiggling about in every direction. When he couldn't hold it inside any longer, he burst out laughing.

'Hahahahaha! It tickles *so* much!' he howled. 'Make it stop! *Hahahahaha! Make it stop!*'

Blossom was also in a fit of hysterics. Tears were running down her cheeks as if someone had told her the funniest joke she'd ever heard.

The hilarity of it all was so infectious that it set Bruno and Rocco off again. Soon they were all laughing so hard they thought their sides were going to split.

They were laughing and howling and screaming so loudly they almost didn't hear Dottie barking at them.

'Hey! Cut it out, you guys!'

'OK, OK,' said Jack. Then he came to his senses.

'What was that?' he asked Dottie, as if he had misheard her somehow.

'Did you hear that?' Blossom said. 'Did Dottie just …'

'Stop messing about, will you!' Dottie barked again, louder this time. 'I've discovered something! I've been trying to tell you! There's something behind the ivy!'

'What did you say?' Jack gasped in shock, wiping the tears from his cheeks.

'Did she just speak?' Blossom said with her mouth hanging open like a codfish.

'What are you two on about?' Bruno said, still laughing as if it was some kind of joke.

'There's something behind the ivy downstairs!' Dottie barked again. 'I can smell it!'

'Can you hear that?' Jack said. 'She's

telling us she can smell something!'

'What do you mean she's telling you?' laughed Rocco. 'Stop messing about!'

But Jack wasn't laughing, and neither was Blossom. They were staring at Dottie in shock.

'Can you not hear her?' Jack asked.

'*No!*' Bruno cried. 'All we can hear is you two going nuts!'

'I can hear her too!' cried Blossom. 'I can understand her! I can really understand what she's saying!'

'Can you understand us, Dottie?' asked Jack.

'Of course I can!' barked Dottie. 'Now come on …' she said,

bounding off down the stairs.

Blossom and Jack ran after her, though
Bruno flashed past them in a blur and
Rocco swooped down from above long
before they got there. Dottie was barking
excitedly at the wall of ivy, and sniffing
madly at the leaves.

'I can smell fresh water,' Dottie barked.
'Mountain air and sweet apricots!'

'What's she saying?' asked Bruno,
furious to be left out of the conversation.

Dottie was still scrabbling away at the
wall of ivy in the sheer hope of discovering
an opening, a hole, a crack … something!

Then Dottie barked again, one final
time, loudly.

'What did she say that time?' asked
Rocco.

Blossom and Jack turned to look at each
other, their eyes like saucers.

'She's saying …' started Jack, not quite

able to believe what he was about to say. 'She's saying it's another world ...' he finished.

'Should we look?' asked Blossom.

Jack nodded. He walked over to the wall, his heart pounding, unsure of what he might find.

Slowly, he pulled back the vines.

But there was nothing behind them but a brown brick wall.

A MARVELLOUS IDEA!

The secret summer gang came out of the strange room and back into the entrance hall. Jack was unsure if he felt relieved or disappointed.

It seemed like days since he had walked in there that morning – and he knew he had to go home. If his dad came back and found him out of the house at this hour he'd be in so much trouble.

The gang parted ways swiftly, unsure what to make of their new powers, or what it all meant. They all agreed to sleep on it, and meet early the next day.

Giant rolling clouds had formed in the sky, and the rain was coming down heavily now. By the time Jack had made it across his garden to the back door, his clothes were drenched.

To Jack's relief, his dad wasn't home yet, so he ran upstairs to dry off and change into his pyjamas, then came back down to the kitchen again. He put the radio on and made himself a jam sandwich, and one for his dad.

The news about the storm was spreading like wildfire. Streams and rivers had already begun rising due to the heavy rainfall and apparently the worst was yet to come.

The house was very quiet as Jack made his way up the stairs again with his sandwich. It was getting late but Jack had too much on his mind to feel tired.

He opened the window so he could hear

the sound of the rain. It had calmed a little now, and the night air was warm. The light of the moon shone through Jack's window on to the bed where he sat. He was thinking hard about the clues they had found, but it was as if there was a piece of the puzzle missing. And that piece was Blossom's dad.

Out of nowhere, a small head suddenly popped up from beneath the window and said, 'Hey, kid!'

Jack almost leapt off the bed in shock as Blossom hopped up and landed perfectly on the window ledge.

'How did you get up here?' Jack asked, coming over to the window. 'Come in, you're getting wet.'

'I climbed up the drainpipe.' She shrugged.

Jack gazed up at her in wonder. With her pale face set against the dark night outside, and framed by the open window, she looked as if she was in a mysterious painting.

Jack helped her into the room. Blossom began staring around at all his things.

'Is this where you sleep?' she asked him.

Jack nodded. There were no lights on and the room was very dark. But the moon was full and cast its silvery light across the walls.

Blossom perched on the edge of his bed. She was gazing at the wall covered with all of Jack's postcards.

'They're from my mum,' he told her. 'She sends them from the places she visits.'

There was a short silence.

'Do you miss her?' Blossom asked.

'I suppose so,' said Jack. 'Though I don't really remember her.' Then after a pause he asked, 'Do you miss your dad?'

As soon as he had said this, Jack's tummy went all tight and he immediately regretted his words. Of course she missed him. It was a silly question.

Blossom gazed out of the window. 'I do,' she said, 'even though I can't remember him. The same as you, I suppose.'

Jack nodded. 'It's weird because I never really knew her. But I can feel her, as if she's still here. I sometimes wonder if I'll ever see her again,' he said, 'but as I get older, I realise that's probably just wishful thinking.'

His words quietly disappeared out of the window and into the night.

'I'm sure you'll see her again one day,' said Blossom quietly.

'And I'm sure you'll see your dad,' said Jack with a faint smile.

Blossom picked up the postcard from the stool next to Jack's bed. 'Where's this?' she asked.

'That's Paris,' said Jack. 'That building's

called the Eiffel Tower. I imagine she's still
there because it only arrived a couple of
days ago and Paris isn't that far away.'

Blossom was staring closely at the card,
frowning at something as she held it up in
the pale moonlight. Then she put it back on
the stool.

'Anyway!' said Blossom. 'I came to see
you because I have had a marvellous
idea ...' She turned to him, her green eyes
shining. 'I was wondering, do you think the
animals at the home where your dad works
might know where my dad is?'

'What do you mean?' said Jack.

'Well, it seems as if my dad knows a
lot about animals,' she said. 'So maybe he
worked there too? Or at least went there
a lot? How else would he know all that
stuff – all their little quirks and secrets – if
he hadn't spent lots of time with them?
And there can't be *too* many elephants in

town, surely …'

'But how would that help?' Jack asked. 'I mean, he's not there now, is he?'

'Well,' said Blossom, 'now we can speak to animals, we can go and ask them where he's gone!'

Jack looked at her. Then he started giggling. The thought was just too funny. But then he noticed that her face didn't change, and it suddenly began to dawn on him.

'You're not being serious?' he said to her.

'I am,' she replied defiantly.

Jack began shaking his head in confusion. 'We're going to ask the animals where your dad is?'

'Well, why can't we?' she said, throwing her arms in the air. 'We can talk to Dottie!'

'That's a crazy idea!' Jack cried. 'What if someone sees us?'

Blossom grinned at him. Jack couldn't help the tiniest flicker of a smile appearing on his face too.

Blossom clearly took that as a yes. She leapt up into the air with a whispered cry of joy.

'We are going to have to be careful,' said Jack in a serious voice.

Blossom nodded at him, trying to look serious too, but failed to conceal the joy in her eyes.

'We can't let my dad see we're there,' he went on, 'or get caught by his boss Mr Nettles, or we could get my dad into big trouble.'

'Deal!' said Blossom with a firm nod. 'We are the secret summer gang after all, so it wouldn't be right if we didn't do it in secret.'

She held out her hand and Jack shook it.

'Till tomorrow then!' she said as she

climbed back out on to the window ledge and went sliding down the drainpipe as if it were one of the vines in her magical home.

Jack remained sitting on his bed for a moment, smiling to himself. He glanced down at the postcard that was on the stool. Blossom had left it with the message facing up. And as the moonlight shone down on it, that was when Jack noticed something.

He was staring at the back of the card. But he wasn't looking at the message written on it. He was looking at the top right corner. There was no stamp on it. There was nothing there at all.

His head flicked to the wall of postcards and he could feel his heart beating inside his chest.

He stood up slowly and walked towards the wall. A frightful sense of panic came over him as he reached out and plucked one off the wall. He turned the card over and looked on the back. No stamp.

He reached out and grabbed another. There was no stamp on that one either. His breathing was getting louder and faster and he began tearing all the cards off the wall. His fingernails were scraping away at all the stuck-down corners and the postcards rained down on him like leaves from a withering tree.

Once they were all off the wall, Jack knelt on the floor and sifted through them. His hands were shaking and his stomach was twisting itself into painful knots. It was then that Jack became aware of another presence in the room. He lifted his head and there silhouetted in the doorway was his father.

178

MR BROOM'S
SECRET

Jack's father came into the room and sat
down on the small chair in the corner with
a sigh.

There was a long silence.

'The postcards,' said Jack. 'They're not
from her, are they?'

Jack knew. Somehow, a part of him had
always known.

'No, they're not,' his father said. 'I wrote
them. I wrote them all. I've delivered every
single one to you since you were a toddler.
I thought about stopping after a while. But
you loved them.'

Mr Broom smiled sadly to himself and as the moon shone against the side of his face, little glints of light sparkled in his eyes.

'You loved seeing all the pictures,' he chuckled, 'learning about all the different places. Somehow it made it seem as if she was still here with us. Made me think she was coming back – and like you, I'm still hoping. Still waiting for that marvellous day to come.'

'Did she leave because of me?' asked Jack.

'How could you even ask something like that?' said Mr Broom. 'You don't really think that, do you?'

Jack thought for a moment. It had always been a question that existed somewhere in the back of his mind.

'I don't know what to think,' said Jack quietly.

'I wish I could explain to you what

happened,' his father said. 'But the simple truth is, I don't know myself. It's always been a mystery.'

The skin all over Jack's body had turned cold as he waited for his father to continue.

'I suppose you're old enough to know now. The truth is, Jack,' Mr Broom went on, 'I don't know what happened to your mum. She went looking for your granddad. He hadn't turned up to work for some time, so she was worried. That's what she told me anyway. Perhaps she was looking for an excuse. A way out. I'll never know. Because she never came back.'

There was a small crack in Mr Broom's voice.

'Your mum never wanted to move back to this place. She wanted to travel. To see the world. She grew up here, did you know that?'

Jack shook his head.

'We only moved back because she was worried about your granddad. I guess once he was gone, she decided to take her chance. I always hoped she would return one day, but she never did.'

'So she just … disappeared?' Jack whispered.

'I'm sorry I never told you,' said Mr Broom, staring into Jack's eyes with great sadness. 'I was just trying to protect you.'

Mr Broom watched Jack in the darkness. Jack knew he was waiting for him to say something. But he didn't know what to say.

His dad sighed, and a moment later slowly rose out of his chair.

'I'll leave you now,' he said. 'If you need me, I'll be downstairs. I'm heading to work early tomorrow.'

Then his father walked out of the room, closing the door softly behind him.

Jack sat there listening to his father's

footsteps travelling down the stairs. Then everything was silent, and Jack found himself alone once more.

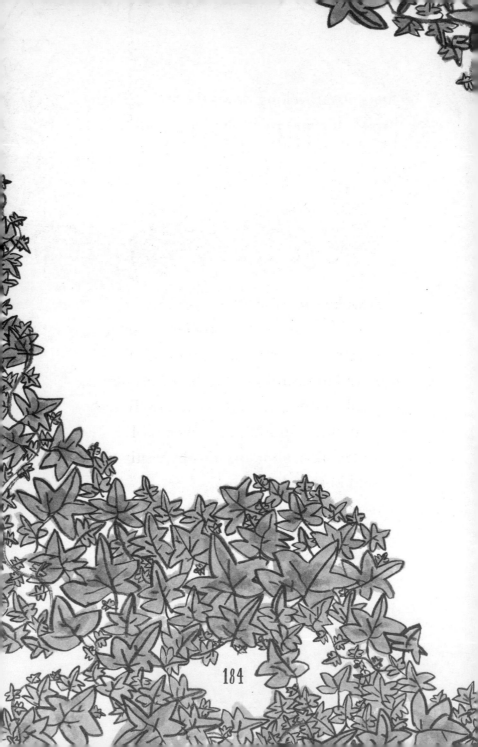

THE ANIMAL HOME

Jack woke early the next morning.

He felt a sadness somewhere inside him as his strange conversation with his father replayed in his mind. But there was no time to think about that mystery today. Today the gang had another mystery to solve, and they were going to start by visiting the animal home.

So Jack pushed the feeling down, dressed quickly, then knocked on the Buckleys' front door to tell them the plan.

'I can fly there!' Rocco cried, excited at the thought.

'Well, you'd better get going then!'
said Bruno to his brother. 'It will only
take me about thirty seconds with my
cheetah speed, so you'll need a head start!'

'Oh please!' said Rocco, rolling his eyes.
'I've got wings, baby – so I'll be *way* faster
than you.'

An hour later, Jack and Blossom were
standing on the edge of the hill looking out
over the town.

'You ever ridden a bike before?' Jack
asked.

Blossom shrugged. 'I can't remember.'

'Well, don't worry,' Jack said to her. 'You
can just stand on the back of mine.'

'How does that work?' she asked him.

'I'll show you,' said Jack and then
suddenly paused.

'Is that my T-shirt?' he asked her.

Blossom stared down at it guiltily.

'Sorry,' she said. 'I needed a fresh one and I saw it on the washing line.'

Jack rolled his eyes, but couldn't help smiling. 'Keep it,' he said.

'Thanks,' said Blossom sheepishly, as she tried to hide a large yawn. 'I'm tired. Too many late days. I hope I don't fall asleep on the way.'

'I wouldn't worry,' said Jack. 'The ride down should perk you up a bit.'

The rain seemed to have stopped for a while at least, and a beam of sunlight had even managed to break through the thick grey clouds that filled the sky.

Everywhere in the town neighbours were hanging out of their windows in deep discussion, saying things like, 'Such miserable weather!' and, 'Where's our summer gone?'

Jack's bike was a red BMX. It had bright yellow handlebars and huge knobbly black

tyres. On the axle of the rear wheel there
were two short metal pegs sticking out on
each side.

'What are those for?' Blossom asked
with a tilted head.

'You're going to stand on them,' said
Jack.

Blossom folded her arms and replied,
'How about *you* stand on them?'

Jack paused briefly, then nodded as
Blossom came forward and leapt up on to
the saddle.

'I've never stood on the back before,'
said Jack as he climbed up on to the pegs
and rested his hands upon Blossom's
shoulders. 'It's actually quite comfy.'

'You ready?' said Blossom with her eyes
half closed.

'You bet,' Jack replied. 'Now don't go
too fast. The back brake is a little loose.'
But before Jack had even finished the

sentence, Blossom had released her fingers from the brake and they went shooting down the hill like a rocket!

Within seconds, they had started to gather incredible speed. They were going so fast that when Jack opened his mouth, his cheeks puffed out into a ginormous ball and his lips were flapping about wildly like a happy dog sticking its head out of the window of a moving car. He held on tight to Blossom's shoulders as the wind went whipping past them.

Jack closed his eyes and smiled. It felt as though they were flying. When he opened them again, he saw they were overtaking a large bus filled with goggle-eyed passengers. Every face on the bus was pushed up against the glass as they all marvelled at Blossom and Jack whizzing by.

Jack pointed upwards, to a small dot high up in the sky above them.

'It's Rocco!' Jack shouted.

The hill was soon far behind them and they were now surrounded by rows of houses and local shops on all sides. They passed a grocery store, the post office and the bakery.

'Hey, that's the bakery!' said Blossom, breathing in the wonderful smell. 'Mmm, cake …'

'I sometimes go there with my dad,' said Jack, hoping that wasn't the wrong thing to say.

All across town, the streets were empty. People had obviously decided to stay in due to the horrible weather.

They finally arrived at a large park and, beyond it, Jack could see the animal home.

When they arrived, Bruno was already there.

'You took your time,' he said as Jack tied his bike to the metal railings by the entrance.

'Where's Rocco?' asked Blossom.

'He's already inside,' Bruno said. 'I'm gonna whizz through now while there's no one in the booth … catch you in there!' And in a flash, Bruno had shot off in a dizzying blur.

'I love it when he does that,' said Jack as he and Blossom headed over to the ticket booth, which did indeed seem to be empty.

'Hello?' said Jack, peering in through the glass.

A strange hoarse voice spoke out from the depths of the booth, saying, 'How many tickets?'

'Hello, my name's Jack and I've come to see my dad, who works here. Mr Broom?'

A moment later a head popped up. 'Oh, you're Jack, are you?' said a peculiar-looking woman with a mop of purple tangly hair resting on her head. 'Albert's son! I haven't seen you since you were tiny. You probably don't even remember me, do you? Mrs Pog?'

Jack didn't remember her, but he smiled anyway. She had a friendly face that was caked in layers of thick colourful make-up which made her whole head shine like a magnificent rainbow.

'What are you kids doing here on a day like this?' she said. 'You know there's a big storm on the way? You don't wanna get struck by lightning, do you? Might sting a bit!'

She winked at the pair then released the barrier.

The animal home was usually a very busy place at this time of year. On any normal summer's day, it would be crowded with families and happy children all giggling and gawping at the animals,

holding ice lollies or bags of
sweets.

Thanks to the weather, there
wasn't anyone around at all. And
yet Jack and Blossom could hear what
seemed to be hundreds of voices.

Except these weren't human voices.
These voices belonged to the animals.

As Jack and Blossom wandered further
into the animal home, strange and
peculiar mutterings from all around filled
their ears.

'Can you hear that?' Jack said.

'It's almost deafening …' Blossom
whispered.

They passed a large emu who was
looking out at them from its pen. It seemed
very confused and its head was twitching in
every direction.

'Do you think my head is too small
for my body?' it said to them in a

panicked voice.

Jack and Blossom stared at the strange creature, lost for words.

'It is, isn't it,' the emu said. 'That's why you're not saying anything. I look ridiculous, don't I? They don't even give us haircuts in this place.'

'I think you look great!' Blossom said, shrugging her shoulders.

'Really?' said the emu. 'You're not just saying that?'

They walked on and two seagulls suddenly swooped down and landed on a bench just in front of them. One had an empty chip packet dangling from its beak and the other seemed very cross about it indeed.

'You never save any for me, do you! Ohhhh noooooo … ! You've always got to have it allllll to yourself!'

'Oh, here he goes!' the other one piped

up. 'Do you ever stop whinging?'

'Would it kill you to leave me one measly chip? Just one?'

The plumper of the two seagulls then squawked something unrepeatable in the other one's face and flew off.

Jack and Blossom looked and listened in amazement.

They could hear every single creature they passed. Every chirp and squeak and squawk and growl was a word spoken or a comment thrown from one animal to another. It was incredible. The monkeys were moaning and the llamas were laughing. There wasn't a creature in there that didn't have *something* to say.

'We need to find the elephant,' said

Jack. 'Remember your dad's note in the encyclopaedia? He said elephants told him stories and that they remember everything. So if this elephant ever spoke to your dad, he'll definitely remember!'

Blossom nodded. As they passed the next enclosure, she looked up towards the branches of a tree and called out, 'Excuse me? Do you know where we might be able to find the elephants?'

Jack followed her gaze, expecting to see a bird up there, and was surprised instead to see a giraffe stretching its long neck towards the treetop and tearing itself off some delicious leaves.

It chewed thoughtfully for a moment before answering. 'Elephants …' the giraffe said. 'There's only one elephant around here. Make a left up ahead, then keep going, towards the far east corner.

You'll find him over there – big enclosure, wooden gate. Can't miss it.' And with a nod, the giraffe reached for another mouthful of leaves, and went back to chewing.

Blossom turned to Jack and said, 'Well, that was easy enough!'

They walked on until they reached the left turn, which led them up a long winding pathway, past various enclosures whose animals seemed to want to stay hidden. Eventually up ahead they saw a wooden gate, and behind it a huge, grassy field. Blossom immediately leapt over the fence and disappeared into the grass.

'Wait for me!' said Jack, trying to keep up.

By the time he'd got over the fence and

made it into the field, Blossom was nowhere to be seen. He walked on up the gently sloping field till at last he caught sight of her.

Like a lioness nestled in the tall grass, Blossom was silently hunting her prey, moving slowly through the field. Then suddenly she stopped, sat cross-legged on the grass in front of a wall of green bushes, and waited.

He crouched down beside her.

'What are you looking at?'

'Watch,' she whispered.

They waited silently.

There was a rustling noise. Then came the deep thundering of giant footsteps. Jack held his breath as the footsteps got louder and the leaves of the bushes began to quiver until suddenly a huge elephant came striding through.

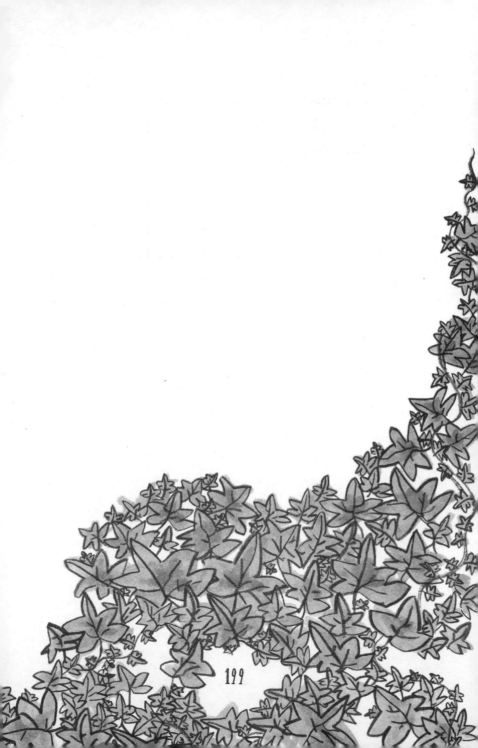

199

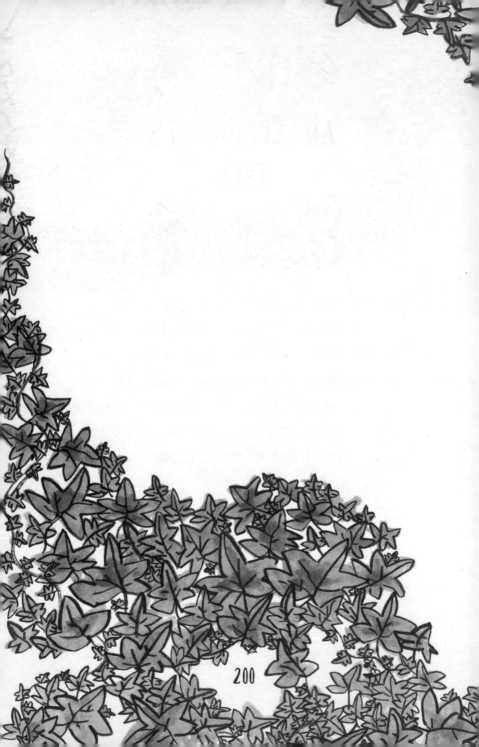

AN ELEPHANT'S TALE

What a most magnificent-looking creature the elephant is. This one was as big as a bus and had a long thick trunk with giant cream-coloured tusks on either side. His grey skin was wrinkled all over and as thick as leather. The ears were ginormous and a great tuft of frizzy silvery hair was growing out of the top of his head.

As the great elephant came slowly towards them, Jack could feel his whole body beginning to tremble. He had never felt so excited and afraid all at the same time.

The creature was looking carefully at Blossom as his tail flicked through the air like a sweeping broom.

'Are you going to say something to him?' Jack whispered out of the side of his mouth.

Blossom didn't answer him. She seemed remarkably calm.

Then, before either of them had a chance, the elephant spoke.

'I know you,' he said in a deep, rich voice.

Jack drew in a sharp breath.

He couldn't quite believe what was happening. The elephant was actually speaking to them.

'Have we met before?' Blossom asked the elephant.

The elephant gazed at her for a few moments with his tail still swishing back and forth.

'Yes we have,' he said softly. 'My name is Jumbo.'

'I like that name,' said Blossom. 'My name is Blossom and this is Jack.'

Jack's heart now seemed to be lodged inside his throat. He looked around to check nobody was watching, which nobody was. There wasn't another person in sight.

Jumbo spoke with a voice that came from a different time. 'What brings you here on such a miserable day?'

'We thought you could help us,' said Blossom. 'I'm searching for my dad. We think he worked here a long time ago and that maybe he was a friend of yours?'

Jumbo continued staring at the two children with his round black eyes. They were like enormous shining marbles. Then, very slowly, he lowered his body on to the grass and sat down with a *thump!* Jack had never seen an elephant sit down before.

The elephant swished his large trunk happily and seemed very comfortable in his new position. 'Go on,' he said.

'We found some notes scribbled in the back of a book,' Jack said, finally having found his voice. 'They said that elephants have powerful memories and that they can tell stories.'

Not a muscle moved in the elephant's face as he watched them.

'Do you remember speaking with anyone before us?'

It suddenly struck Jack how worn and tired the elephant looked and he wondered how old Jumbo actually was. However, he thought it impolite to ask such a question and instead waited patiently for the elephant to respond.

'There was only one human I spoke with,' said the elephant. 'It was many years ago when I met him, though I remember it as if it were yesterday.'

Blossom's eyes lit up. 'So it's true – elephants never forget!' she said.

'So they say,' the aged elephant replied with a chuckle.

'Do you remember what this human looked like?' asked Blossom.

'I do,' said the elephant. 'This was also the human I met you with.'

Blossom looked at Jack with delight. Then she turned to Jumbo the elephant. 'Tell us everything!' she pleaded.

'I was only a baby when I first came here. I arrived with a damaged leg. An unfortunate start in life, some might say. My disability has always prevented me from being able to survive in the wild. So, they kept me here.'

Jack and Blossom listened in a trance, hardly daring to move.

'I never really minded humans much.

I saw them as reasonably competent and a kind-natured sort of breed. The humans here have always cared for me. But there was one human who was different.'

'Why were they different?' asked Jack. He could barely swallow he was so excited.

'The funny thing with humans is, they never hear you,' the elephant continued. 'You can be trying to tell them something until you are blue in the face, but they'll never listen. And then, one day, this human began taking care of me. We spent many years together and slowly, over time, he learned to hear me. He learned to hear my voice and he became my friend.'

'He could understand what you were saying?' asked Blossom.

The elephant gently nodded.

'He must have swallowed one of the magic gobstoppers like we did!' said Jack.

The elephant shook his head and

laughed. 'I'm afraid you are mistaken. The magic you speak of wasn't given to him. He didn't swallow it. He learned it. He *created* it … He made the magic himself!'

'I knew it!' Blossom gasped.

'The human and I learned to talk to each other. He had all sorts of inventions in mind. The idea of memories is the one he was toying with the most.'

'Memories?' Blossom said.

'The power of my memory was of extraordinary interest to him. The human began by taking a single tear from my eye. He would collect these tears over time and mix them into magic potions, keeping them in tiny little bottles. He had this crazy notion of giving humans back their memories. Not just any memory, but their most perfect and happiest one. Literally returning them to that place and allowing

207

them to re-live the moment all over again as if it were happening for the very first time. However, there were glitches – sometimes people lost their memories, or worse. He never gave up though, and soon he moved on to other animals and created more and more magical potions, or so I heard, harnessing the power of the animals he befriended. But he always came back and spent time with me, until the day he told me he was leaving.'

'What did he say?' asked Blossom.

'He told me he was going to another world.'

At exactly that moment, there was a small rumble in the sky. The thick rolling clouds had blackened once more, casting an enormous shadow over the field.

'Did he say anything about a storm?' asked Jack.

There was a short pause.

'The last great storm arrived six years ago. It was the sixth of February. A dark day. The heavens opened and the rain poured down for days on end. The human came to me through the thunder and the lightning. What he said didn't make much sense. He was raving, as he often did. He said the bottles had fallen in the storm, and the magic had spilled and mixed, and from it a great garden had grown. When the storm watered that garden, a doorway to another world would appear ... and he said he was going to go through. He promised he would come back and take me with him, but that was the last time I saw him.'

Blossom's eyes shone with hope and tears as she spun round to Jack.

'It's the storm!' she cried urgently. 'That's what opens the doorway, the one that Dottie can smell. And that's why Dad hasn't come back. The doorway hasn't opened yet! My dad's found another world and there hasn't been a big enough storm to bring him home again!'

'It must have been the bottles that created it, the ones you found on the floor …' said Jack, still trying to piece together what the elephant had told them.

'I knew he wouldn't leave me! I have to get back to the house!' She leapt up on to her feet. 'I can't miss the doorway opening again …' she was yelling as she raced away.

Jack scrambled up too. 'Hey, Blossom, wait!' He was just about to run after her when the elephant spoke to him.

'You know I've met you before too,' said the elephant.

'What? Yes, my dad works here,' said Jack, not wanting to be rude, but desperate to chase after Blossom.

'No, with the girl,' said the elephant.

'What do you mean?' said Jack, confused. 'No, you must be mistaken. I've only just met her.' He added over his shoulder, 'I have to go, I'm sorry.'

Already Blossom was disappearing off into the distance. Jack ran as fast as he could across the grass, hopped back over the fence, and was just about to call out to her when from behind him a strong hand grabbed his shoulder. Jack swung round to see a snarling face glaring right into his eyes.

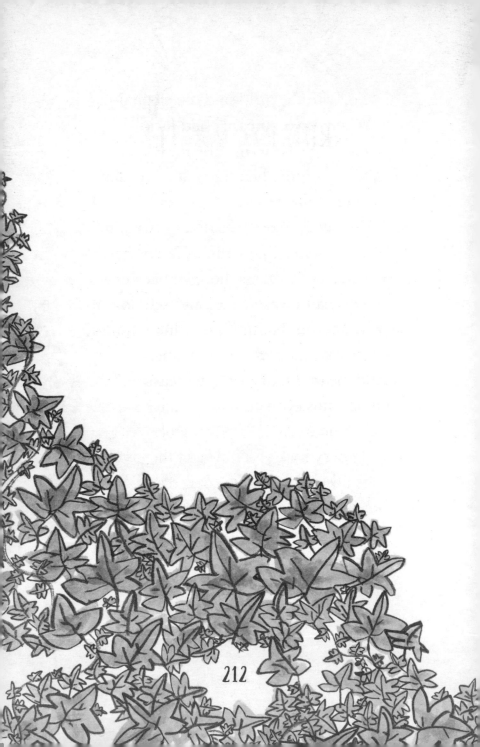

GRUMPY NETTLES

With a sinking heart, Jack realised who it was. It was Mr Nettles, his father's boss.

He was an extremely short person with small, mean eyes, a big bald head and the lumpiest nose you could ever have had the misfortune to lay eyes on. It looked like an old slippery rock you'd find at the bottom of the ocean and as Jack gazed at it, his whole body wriggled with a squirm.

'I want to see your ticket,' said Mr Nettles, clicking his fingers a centimetre away from Jack's nose.

Jack didn't move.

'You don't have one, do you?' said Mr Nettles, his face reddening with fury. 'I thought as much. Sneaked over the wall, did you? Well, I won't allow it! Do you hear me?'

His forehead was all wrinkled with anger and tiny flecks of spit came spraying out of his mouth as he spoke.

'I will not allow this sort of thing to happen while I'm in charge of this place! Not under my roof!'

'There's not a roof on this place, you bumbling buffoon,' came a booming voice from beyond the fence.

Had Jack just heard what he thought he had? He turned his head and there at the fence was Jumbo.

He felt a little smile begin to creep across his lips.

'Why are you smiling?' snapped Mr Nettles. 'Oh, you think this is funny, do you? Well, you won't be laughing when I call your parents. What's your name?'

The smile fell from Jack's face. He didn't want his father to get into trouble.

'I didn't sneak in,' Jack admitted with a sigh. 'My dad works here and the woman at the ticket office let me through.'

'A likely story,' grunted Mr Nettles. 'Do you think I was born yesterday?'

'Of course he doesn't think you were born yesterday,' trumpeted Jumbo again. 'You'd still be a baby if you were born yesterday, you egg-headed moron.'

Jack couldn't help giggling.

'What are you sniggering at, you little toerag?' Mr Nettles screamed at Jack.

'I'd rather you didn't speak to my son like that.'

Jack and Mr Nettles turned to see Mr Broom walking towards them, his giant ring of keys jangling with every step.

He was considerably taller than Mr Nettles and stood there very calmly in his dusty overalls, holding a muddy shovel in his hand.

Mr Nettles composed himself for a moment and stared Mr Broom directly in the eye.

'This is your son, Broom?' he said, puffing out his chest.

'He is,' Mr Broom replied, 'and I don't approve of the way you were speaking to him just now.'

'Well, it certainly seems as if somebody has to give him a talking-to!' Mr Nettles bellowed.

'And what is it my son is being accused of?' asked Mr Broom calmly.

'Sneaking in!' Mr Nettles snapped. 'He entered without a ticket! Entering here without a ticket is a crime!'

Jack glanced up at his father, who was

standing very still.

'And your proof?' Mr Broom asked.

'Proof?' Mr Nettles barked. 'What do you mean, proof? The boy hasn't got a ticket!'

'There must be some kind of explanation,' Mr Broom said. 'I doubt very much my son would have just sneaked in. Perhaps Mrs Pog let him in?'

Mr Broom looked at Jack and Jack nodded.

Mr Nettles stepped forward. He was standing very close to Mr Broom now.

'You don't like me very much, do you, Broom.' His voice was quiet and dangerous, and he spoke with an unpleasant smirk on his face.

'You don't like the way I control things around here. Well, you know what, I don't like you much either. I didn't like your father-in-law, and I definitely don't like you.'

Jack blinked. His father-in-law? Jack's granddad?

'Well, that much is clear,' said Mr Broom. 'I'm going to take my son home now. Come on, Jack.'

But Jack hardly heard him. He was in a daze, trying to piece together how Mr Nettles would know his granddad as his dad grabbed his arm and led him out of the animal home.

220

ANOTHER WORLD

Jack's mind was racing as they drove back in silence. Jack knew he should apologise, but he needed a minute to think …

'What were you *doing* there, Jack? I've told you what Nettles is like. Something like this could lose me my job …'

'I know, Dad, I'm sorry,' said Jack. As the rain beat against the window, Jack knew he was going to have to say something. 'I … I promised my friend I'd take her there. She's … she's by herself, and she's never … seen an elephant before?' Jack finished slightly lamely.

'Who's this friend?' asked Mr Broom. 'Who are you talking about?'

'Blossom,' said Jack. 'Her name is Blossom.'

'Blossom?' said his dad with a startled glance at Jack. He gave a little chuckle.

'What's funny?' Jack said.

'Nothing, really. It's just that's what your granddad used to call your mum when she was a little girl.'

All at once, every nerve inside Jack's body exploded with electricity. He was instantly filled with a swarm of butterflies, but they felt bigger than butterflies – they felt like giant bats flapping away wildly inside his chest, as at last Jack's brain reached for the missing piece.

'Dad,' asked Jack in a quiet voice, 'where did Granddad used to work?'

'He worked at the animal home, of course,' Mr Broom said. 'He was a zoologist. You knew that, didn't you? Your granddad got me this job when we moved here. He was losing his marbles a bit by that point, talking to your mum about how he could speak to the animals. That was just before he went missing.'

Jack's mind was travelling at over a thousand miles per hour.

'And when was that?' Jack asked.

'That was about six years ago now,' said Dad. 'Strangely enough, there was a big storm then too, just like this one.'

He couldn't explain how exactly, but somehow, Jack just knew. Even though it didn't make sense, it was still the only possible explanation.

Blossom's missing dad was Jack's granddad, and Blossom … was Jack's mum.

The note about the storm in Blossom's pocket must have been from his granddad to his mum, and then she'd gone to the old house to look for him, all those years ago, and somehow she'd never come back.

How it came to be that she was nine years old Jack had no idea, but he was certain now that some of the curious magic that had whisked his granddad away from his mum had whisked his mum away too.

His mind was a mess of questions he had no answers for. All he knew for sure was that he had to get to the empty house as quickly as he could.

'I can't lose her again ...' he whispered to himself.

'What's that, son?' Mr Broom said, turning to him.

The black sky was rumbling with thunder now and the rain was getting heavier and heavier.

'Can't you go any faster, Dad?'

'No, Jack, I can't,' replied Mr Broom crossly. 'It's pouring with rain. I can hardly see where I'm going.'

Looking out of the window, Jack could see the trees were now swaying back and forth and the leaves were whizzing through the air like a swarm of angry wasps.

All the houses on top of the hill were shrouded under a blanket of darkness. Great big cracks of lightning lit up the sky. Day had turned into night and the storm had finally arrived.

Jack drummed his fingers impatiently on the dashboard as at last the car finally pulled up outside their house. Before it had even stopped, Jack jumped out and ran off towards the back garden.

'Jack!' his father shouted after him. 'Where are you going?'

Jack sprinted past Mr and Mrs Buckley, who had just arrived back from their holiday and were yelling at Aunt Nora.

'What have you done with all our furniture?' Mrs Buckley was screaming. 'It's soaking wet!'

Bruno and Rocco were watching and laughing. 'Hey, Jacky-boy!' Bruno called out as Jack ran past. But Jack had no time to stop.

The rain pounded down on him and a flash of lightning lit up the sky as Jack raced across his garden, down the alley, through the old rusty gate and into the tunnel that led to the empty house. The door was open and his discarded bike was outside. 'Mum?' he called out without thinking. 'I mean …

Blossom!' he corrected himself as he tore up the stairs two at a time. He had never run as fast as this before.

A whoosh of air suddenly went shooting past him like a bullet and Bruno miraculously appeared at the top of the

stairs in front of him. Then a
voice came yelling from behind. 'Jack,
wait!'

Jack swung round and there was
Rocco too, flying into the house after him.

The three of them went sprinting
together past the staircase that led up to
Blossom's den and on instead into the
room at the back of the house. They
could hear Dottie was already in
there, barking madly at the ivy.

Jack gasped as they entered the
room and looked over at the
back wall.

Because there
wasn't a wall
there any more.
From behind the thick
curtain of vines, great
glimmers of golden light
were shining through.

Another rumble of thunder boomed out, followed by a great bolt of lightning that struck the house and the glimmering light behind the ivy flashed and sparkled.

Jack shielded his eyes as he took a shaky step towards it. Very slowly, he reached out his hand and parted the ivy with the tips of his fingers. The sparkling light spilled through the leaves and a breath of warm air gently touched the skin on his face. It smelled sweet.

'See? Apricots!' barked Dottie. She was wagging her tail like mad.

Jack looked down. Just beyond his feet he could see soft green grass.

The warm bright light was glittering all around them.

'What should we do?' asked Bruno.

Jack breathed in deeply and looked at the brothers. There was so much he couldn't explain to them right now. But he knew one thing for certain.

'We promised we'd help Blossom find her dad,' he said, 'so that's what we should do.'

Bruno and Rocco looked at each other for a moment. Then they glanced back at Jack, and nodded.

And together they they all stepped through into another world.

ACKNOWLEDGEMENTS

First and foremost, an enormous thank you to two people who helped me write this book. Anne McNeil, and my glorious editor, Lily Morgan. Words will never be able to express my gratitude to you both.

A very special thank you to Alice McKinley who made this story so much more with her beautiful illustrations and to the amazing team at Hachette Children's Group – Alice Duggan, Felicity Highet, Becci Mansell, Jennifer Hudson, and everyone else involved.

Thank you to my copyeditor Becca Allen, and my proofreader Catherine Coe.

Thank you to my brilliant agent Sam Day.

And most importantly of all, my eternal love and thanks to my beautiful Ella. I love you darling girl.

Jack's Secret World

Coming March 2021!

Jack Ryder was cast in the role of Jamie Mitchell in *EastEnders* at the age of sixteen – a character he played for five years. He then moved into theatre, performing in plays by Alan Bennett, Tim Firth and David Hare, before going on to direct the West End productions of *Calendar Girls* and *The Band* musical. It is his lifelong ambition to be a children's book author. *Jack's Secret Summer* is his first book.